LUNA STATION
QUARTERLY

Issue 030 | June 2017

Editor-in-Chief

Jennifer Lyn Parsons

Assistant Editors

Tara Calaby • Cathrin Hagey • Dana Mele
Andi Marquette • Megan Patton
Danielle Perry • Iona Sharma

LUNA STATION PRESS
NEW JERSEY

First Paperback Edition June 2017

ISBN: 978-1-938697-85-2

Luna Station Quarterly publishes short fiction on March 1st, June 1st,
September 1st, and December 1st. For more information and submission
guidelines, please visit our website at lunastationquarterly.com

For Luna Station Press
Creative Director–Tara Quinn Lindsey
Editor-in-Chief & Founder–Jennifer Lyn Parsons

LUNA STATION PRESS

576 Valley Road #197
Wayne, NJ 07470

www.lunastationpress.com

info@lunastationpress.com

CONTENTS

Editorial

Jennifer Lyn Parsons

A pixel-slinger and code monkey by trade, Jennifer is a life-long lover of story with a capital S. Her work has been seen in various magazines and she has published three books, with quite a few more in her back pocket. She counts Jim Jarmusch and Laura Ingalls Wilder as two of her biggest influences. Make of that what you will.

When not writing either code or fiction, she reads books and comics, and sometimes makes things out of wool or paper. She finds joy in making things, be they digital or analog.

Change, whether it comes by choice or not, is always an opportunity to reasses your world and how you live in it. As a writer, this is a prime chance to gather plenty of that "inspiration" stuff everyone is always talking about. It's harder, by far, to do this in the midst of major change in one's life. Moving house, for example, opens up all those hidden bits of yourself you've tucked away in boxes and now must decide if they are worth the burden of their physical as well as their emotional weight. "Does this thing still serve me? Does it bring something into my life?" is a common question I'm asking myself as I sit here at the kitchen table, surrounded by an ocean of boxes.

But beyond the things that we carry, change is a time to reflect on who we have been for the span of time before this and who we want to become moving forward. As the world around us is in upheaval and change is coming at us hard, fast, unbidden, and undesired, we all have that chance to take stock. Who have we been all this time leading up to this moment? Is that person still who we want to be? Can we even still be those people in the face of what is going on in the world around us?

Massive change is also, for better or worse, a chance to stay stagnant, set in ones ways, to resist becoming the next, hopefully better, versions of ourselves. I personally feel that, for all of us, resisting inner evolution is counter-productive. How can we grow if we do not change? How do we become better writers, editors, poets, better people, if we push back against an opportunity for growth? Resisting that kind of inner growth has, in my experience, often ended in the choice being made for me, for the power to choose to be taken out of my hands. The world does not stop spinning and moving and others around us will make choices without us if we choose to stand still.

So, to briefly wrap these thoughts together because there are boxes yet to pack, I leave you with this: What is holding you back in your life? What needs to change? And what can you do to make that move before the world comes sweeping in and decides to force your hand and your options become limited?

The characters featured in the tales to follow face hard choices. They too are in the process of remaking who they are, some by choice, others not. Change and growth go hand in hand, sometimes painful, sometimes joyful, sometimes hard won. These characters know this all too well.

What needs to change in your life? Who do you want to be next? Go grab it with both hands. After all, we have guides to lead the way. We already have stories to show us how it's done.

L S Q | 030

And the White Breast of the Dim Sea

Hilary M. Biehl

Hilary Biehl writes poems and short fiction. She lives in New Mexico with her husband and a 3-year-old wizard who refuses to wear pants.

The tree stands away from the shore, amid wild grasses and abandoned sand-burrows. Untouched by water, the sand here is white and hot. I have to wear shoes simply to stand on it.

The tree gives me things. Clothing, food, jewelry, books. It gave me these shoes. It doesn't ask what I need or what I want; it assumes. If I don't visit for a while, I'll come back to find crumpled silks around the roots and the remains of fruits and cakes scavenged by birds. Sometimes, rarely, a bird comes to sit in the tree and looks at me with my father's eyes.

When I was born my father built a house, not with magic but with his hands. He made it from bags of sand, stuck together and insulated with mud, then covered with sealskin. At high tide the sea came right up to the door; sometimes it brought my mother with it. She was still female, then, Eiryn of the Mergyndr.

My father, Idris, came from a line of enchanters in which all the firstborn were sons. I was not a son: I broke the line. The magic would be lost. Still, my parents loved me. They called me Lotl, a name not Mer or human, and raised me between worlds on the border of the sea.

I used to play knee-deep in the freezing gray water while my father sat on the rocks reading. His feet were bare and his long beard rippled in the wind. Sometimes I'd stop splashing and shrieking long enough to hear one of the spells he muttered to himself compulsively. My mother would surface in the distance, wave to me, and at sunset her shoal would lie in the strange light on a nearby island and sing. We'd listen to them, my father and I. Once when I was about five, I said, "They're singing to me!" He shook his head. "The mergyndr sing for each other, no one else."

"But I'm half mergynd," I said. He only shook his head again.

When I was eleven, fish started dying. No one knew why. Perhaps it had something to do with the huge metal ships that sailed past, dumping trash and spilling oil into the water. In any case, it caused a famine, and some desperate sharks attacked the mergyndr. Several males in my mother's shoal were killed, so she, along with three or four other mature females, filled the void. Her tail turned from white to black and silver, her shoulders broadened, and she became Eirynd.

My father was angry, but most of all he was embarrassed. "How could you?" he demanded. "How could you do it?"

"You knew this would happen," said Eirynd. "It's our way."

"There are other females," said Idris. "You could have stayed a woman, for my sake."

"I've never been a woman," said Eirynd sharply, "any more than I'm a man now. If you thought otherwise, then you deceived yourself."

"And what about Lotl? She's to have two fathers and no mother?"

"Like every mergynd that ever lived," retorted Eirynd. "I'm still her mother in every way that matters. She had my milk when she was young. She doesn't need it now."

Idris looked at me. It was night, and the moon shone on his hair, leaving his face dark. I couldn't tell if he was looking at me with love or disgust. "I guess she doesn't need me either," he said. Early in the morning, he packed his books and left.

Eirynd was furious. "This is a human practice," he said, "to abandon one's offspring. A mergynd who did this would be abandoned in turn by the shoal, given up to sharks. But human men don't think they need shoals to protect them ... that's the problem."

At Eirynd's request, the mergynd enchanter sent gulls inland as spies. Idris, we learned, had consulted with a mage. The question? Whether a half-breed daughter really counted as a firstborn. The mage said that it didn't. If Idris married a human woman, he would have a son to carry on the magic. I might as well not exist.

I asked Eirynd if that was true. "I don't know," he said. "I know very little about human magic. Possibly it molds to human prejudice."

One month after his departure, my father came back. I hugged him, crying, but he hadn't come to stay. He'd come to plant a seedling.

Silent, numb, I watched him dig up the soft white sand. "Come on, Lotl," he said with a smile, "help me." I shook my head. He unbound the seedling's roots and lowered it gently into the hole. "This tree carries an enchantment," he said. "It will look after you, provide whatever you need."

"Have you found a new family yet?" I said.

Idris sighed and looked so pitiable that I wanted to forgive him. But by the time I located the seed of forgiveness, he was gone.

***

"Papa, how many people can have the magic at one time?"

"Only one. When the son, the eldest, understands how to use it, his father simply forgets."

"How old were you when you got it?"

"About seventeen. My father was younger."

"How do you learn to use it?" I was at the age when one can't stop asking questions.

"A need arises," said Idris, "for which no one can provide."

I kept asking, but that's all he would say.

***

It's said that the progeny of a human and a mergynd are sterile, but apparently that's only true when they pair with humans. When I was nineteen, I paired with a mergynd and gave birth to his daughter. The sea owned three quarters of her; we gave her the mername Aniryn. Eirynd's shoal raised her in the water, bringing her to me every two hours at first so that I could nurse her. I'd watch her white pearlescent tail twitch rhythmically as she suckled to sleep, and envy tinged the joy I took in the simplicity of her belonging. Motherhood had not blotted out my need to be someone's child.

By that time, my father had remarried. The gulls reported that he had two children with his new wife: first a son, as the mage had promised, then a girl a little older than Aniryn. He knew about Aniryn's birth, because when I went to the tree I'd find a ball, a teething ring made of wood and leather, a miniature silver spoon. Sometimes I passed the things on to her. Sometimes I just threw them in the sea.

One noon while I was gathering foodstuffs from the tree—bread, apples, cheese, a bottle of port, a ham—a skua settled on one of the branches. It looked straight down at me, as animals do when they're under an enchantment. I looked straight back.

"Why haven't you come to see Aniryn?" I demanded.

"I've been watching her," said the bird.

"But not in person," I said. "You haven't held her, played with her .... She doesn't even know who you are."

"Do you want me to come?"

"Yes."

"Very well," said the bird and flew away.

Not long after that he trudged alone down the bleak hillside, aided by a staff. "Arthritis," he said when he saw me looking at it. He slept in his old bed in the sealskin house; I'd never had a reason to move it. At dawn we went down to the water. I called and Aniryn came on her own, a strong swimmer already.

She showed Idris how she could dive and somersault and hold her breath for long periods underwater. She flopped down on the sand and he ran my old abalone comb through her short, frizzy hair as it dried. I saw how taken he was with her, with her amber eyes and her laugh. But sometimes his look lingered on the little slits and arches at the sides of her neck. Vestigial of course—like dolphins, mergyndr use lungs to breathe—but a reminder of her otherness. I touched the gills on my own neck nervously.

Before he left he sat in the kitchen he'd built, drank the port he'd sent me, and told me about his new children. The boy was nearly seven, funny, good at sports. The girl was blond and given to charming mispronunciations. Although he described them in great detail, it didn't seem to me that either of them were particularly unusual; later, I realized that was the point.

I listened quietly, waiting for him to mention Aniryn. It seemed as if he'd already forgotten her. His body was in my kitchen, but he was less present than when he borrowed a skua's body to watch me. His thoughts had already returned to his other life where things were simple, comfortable, human.

***

At daybreak I lie in the dark, unable to go back to sleep. My legs itch badly; the scales are starting to peel. I walk down to the water, wade into rose-colored light up to my waist. The first sting of saltwater on flaking skin is quickly followed by relief.

A jellyfish's luminous transparency drifts by beneath a reflected cloud. Seal heads silently appear and disappear on the water's surface. The morning is quiet but not still. I know they're out there: Eirynd, Neruynd, Aniryn. I start swimming ... but before I'm halfway to the island, my legs are jelly, my lungs ache. My whole body is weak, inefficient, human. I have just enough strength to get back to the shore.

I sprawl face down on the wet sand, panting in a familiar puddle of loneliness and disappointment.

***

My father came back without my asking, but this time he wasn't alone. His wife wanted to meet me. When I saw her coming, I hunted in my clothes-chest for a scarf to wrap around my neck.

Blodwen was not what I'd expected. She was plump and pretty, with callused hands and muscular arms from working on farms all her life. She was knowledgeable about weather patterns and livestock; she was also an encyclopedia of human social norms and customs, most of which seemed to me completely arbitrary. She insisted on sleeping with me instead of in Idris's bed. I appealed to him with a look, but he only shrugged.

The children had never seen an ocean before. It was low tide, and they were fascinated by the exposed tidepools. Gwilym was seven, Fflur was four. I watched them play together, their fine hair rippling in the wind, blinking spray out of their sea-colored eyes. Nearby Aniryn played with Idris, and I saw the human children throwing glances at her, suspicious and curious.

Blodwen asked me questions. How old was I? Did I see much of my mother's family? (She hesitated over the word "mother.") Was I good at swimming? What did I do all day? Could I read and write? Was I married to Aniryn's father? Evidently Idris hadn't told her much.

"Neruynd was my best friend growing up," I told her.

"Ah," she said. "But ... he would have been a girl back then, isn't that right?"

I nodded.

"And now you have a child together. But you're not married?"

I tried to explain that mergyndr pair monogamously but don't have an additional ceremony for marriage. I could tell that she was trying not to let her feelings on the matter show.

"I'm the village matchmaker," said Blodwen. "Did Idris tell you that? Making marriages is my true passion." She smiled broadly. "I could set you up with a nice young man from our village."

"I'm not like Idris," I said coldly. "I honor my pairing. I won't go running off to some inlander just because Neruynd is tethered to the sea."

I could see that I'd hurt her, and I regretted my words. To soften them, I pulled my skirt up a little. "Besides," I said, "I'm tethered, too. If my legs aren't in saltwater for half the day, they dry out, the scales shed and bleed ..."

I stopped abruptly. She was staring in horror at the pearly enamel on my leg, at the small gaps where skin showed through. Her horror gave me an unfamiliar, perverse pleasure. I pulled off my scarf to show my slitted neck. "You see?" I whispered. "I'm as much like them as like you. My heart has two chambers like a fish. We cold-blooded creatures don't have room to hold all your customs and morals, down there in the deep."

Blodwen shuddered. She stood up, gathered her skirts, and ran away across the sand.

When Neruynd came to collect Aniryn, I told him what I'd said. He laughed. "Your dishonesty's all human."

"You should meet her," I snapped, "so certain she's right about everything, determined to fit our lives and experiences into the mold she's made from hers. She thinks I'm some kind of pervert or fallen woman. I just told her what she wanted to believe."

"And she believed that about the two-chambered heart?" He couldn't stop laughing.

My father didn't find it funny. "What are you doing?" he hissed at me. We were alone on the shore. The others had gone either to the island or the sealskin house. "Why are you playing with her?"

"You're the one playing, not me," I said.

He sighed. "You could come with us, you know. There's a pool near our farm. I could enchant it, make it saltwater. Of course I'd have to move the fish somewhere else ..."

"But this is my home."

Idris studied me. "You'll never fully be one of them, Lotl," he said. "As long as you stay here, you'll be alone."

"I'll be alone anywhere," I told him.

The night was advanced when we went into the house, feeling our way with fingertips along the walls' soft inner curve. Blodwen was sleeping in Idris's bed with both children. I could just make out Gwilym, his hand curled against his cheek in sleep. He had eight, perhaps ten years before the magic would come to him. For the first time I wondered—what if he received it not from Idris, but from me?

I didn't ask myself, then, whether I'd be able to give up the magic voluntarily once I'd grown accustomed to it. I didn't ask whether Gwilym *could* receive the magic, since that had always been assumed. I could only see the possibility. It was like looking at the whole world upside down, or looking at myself turned inside out. What if my mother was right—what if it was only human prejudice that made the magic go from father to son?

After all, I was the firstborn.

***

The evening star is out together with the sun. Murmuring fragments of remembered spells for comfort, I climb over rocks to reach the tree.

I haven't come here in at least a month. I've been living on fish and eel, crab and kelp and bitter tea. Gulls must have eaten most of the food Idris sent; there are several of them around now, on the ground and in the branches. Among the scattered clothes on the ground are some leggings and silk scarves which must have been Blodwen's idea. One scarf hangs from a branch, caught. I pull it down roughly, and the silk tears with a brusque hiss.

One of the gulls is watching me. I turn to face it. "You're not coming back, are you?"

"No," says the gull.

"When the magic goes to Gwilym, then will you come?"

A long silence, ruffled feathers. "I'll make sure that Gwilym knows your needs are to be provided ..."

A surge of anger makes it unexpectedly easy to cut him off. "A need has arisen," I tell him, "for which you can't provide."

Too suddenly for my father to react, the enchantment breaks, leaving everything around me ordinary. The gull flies away, startled. The tree is just a tree. But deep inside me is the tingle of magic, and it sends small shoots like nerve pain into my eyes, my lips, my fingertips, my feet. Magic pools in my lungs, and when I breathe in I can feel them stretch and hold the air like iron.

I walk down to the water. For the first time, there's nothing to hold me back. I keep walking and it rises to my waist, to my chest, to my chin. The water is so cold, I can't tell whether I'm breathing, but it doesn't matter. The air is mine, the water is mine. I can finally disown the land.

The sun, disappearing, makes the wind-scraped waves half black, half bright. Far across them the mergyndr are singing to each other, and to me.

Below the River

Rose Strickman

Rose Strickman is a writer, editor, researcher and all-around fantasy nut living in Seattle, Washington. She therefore believes it is most unfair that she has never seen any mermaids or sirens. Previous publications include "Catfish Princess", "Dragon Hunt", and "Gingerbread Man", among others.

The train journey down was uneventful; Samuel alternated between reading on his smartphone and sleeping fitfully, head rocking against the window. Outside, the landscape shifted smoothly from red-brick suburbs to wide fields to rolling green hills, patched with woodlands.

And rivers, of course: silver-shining, threading the fields and the woods, glittering between rocks and trees, following the train track and the roads like serpents.

Samuel woke up as the train crossed the bridge, rattling and swaying. He opened his eyes blearily to see the glittering surface of the largest river turning dark and transparent in the shadow of the bridge, little rills lacing up rocks. It was beautiful, but he did not try to look at it closely as the train clattered off the bridge and into the town.

At first glance, Elton Bridge had changed little since Samuel's childhood. There were the same deep-shading trees, the same red-brick and wooden-slatted buildings and the broad walkways, the river glimmering through it all. He stared out the window, blinking.

Then he saw his cousin Charlene standing like a grim monument on the platform, her skinny pink-haired daughter beside her, and he was reminded forcibly of how everything was, in fact, vastly different.

He staggered off the train, suitcase a deadweight in his hand, and Charlene's eagle gaze turned in his direction. "Samuel!"

She strode in his direction, the daughter confusedly yanking her earbuds out. "Good to see you, Samuel," Charlene said briskly, giving him a rather gentler hug than she would have in years past. "How was the trip down?"

"Ah, well..." Samuel shrugged. "Okay, I guess." He smiled at the daughter. "Hi, Lenora."

She managed a half-smile, still covertly goggling. "Hi, Uncle Samuel."

How you doing? Samuel was about to say when he suddenly bent in half, racked by an attack of coughs.

Lenora stared, wide-eyed, while Charlene fussed around him. "Your medicine! Did you bring your medicine?"

Slowly, the onslaught eased. Samuel drew one breath, then another. He looked up, hands still braced on his bony knees, to see Charlene still hovering, Lenora gaping, and half the platform staring.

Samuel managed a weak smile. "It's all right, people. I'm fine."

Muttering darkly, Charlene firmly took his suitcase and led him out of the platform to the parking lot. Lenora trailed beside Samuel, eyeing him dubiously.

"Are you really okay?" she asked in an undertone.

"I'm fine for now."

"But you're not—"

"Lenora!" Charlene turned a blazing glower on the teenager. "Don't ask things like that!"

"I was only saying—"

"It's okay, Charlene," Samuel sighed. "Let's just go to the house."

Samuel's things were slung into the trunk, Samuel himself bundled into the passenger seat. Lenora reinserted her earbuds while Charlene, still muttering, started the car.

Once they were in motion, Samuel relaxed somewhat, watching the town go by. The familiar sights—the red-brick library, the bakery where he and Arianne had eaten cookies as children, even the river promenade—were balm. Then they crossed the bridge.

The river was closer beneath this bridge than the one the train used. Closer and darker. A group of kids were wading nearby, but all Samuel could see was the broad dark pool, shaded by the bridge, ringed by rocks, spattered with leaves. For an instant, Samuel thought he could see movement, deep beneath, even though there was no way the doors could be open at this time of day, in this weather.

He looked away, no longer soothed.

***

"So how long have you got?"

Samuel leaned back in his chair with a sigh. On the mantelpiece, the clock ticked, on and on, while outside the river gleamed in the night. "Not long. Six months, more or less. Have you told Lenora?"

"Yes," Charlene said. "But she won't rest until you've confirmed it, you know."

Samuel sighed. "Understandable."

Charlene leaned forward on the sofa, eyes soft as they seldom were. "But, Samuel. Shouldn't you be where you can get treatment easily? Not in this little town."

"Treatments won't do me any good now, Charlene," Samuel said flatly. "It's too late for that. And I wanted to see you again. And...this place." He nodded at the room, at the house that had changed so little in thirty years.

Charlene's gaze hardened. "Are you sure you're not torturing yourself?" she asked, slightly sharp. "It won't bring her back, you know."

Samuel glared. "Yes, Charlene. I do know that. But...I had to come back."

She shook her head, standing up to go to the table and pour them both another amber glassful of whisky. "Well, I guess you know what you're doing. But I hope you're not making a mistake."

So do I. He accepted his glass, felt the drink in his throat like fiery gold. "I'll be trying to finish my book here as well," he said. "So I won't be in your way."

"Don't worry about that," said Charlene. "God knows I had enough practice when George was alive...I'll tell Lenora to keep quiet."

Samuel laughed slightly. "Let her slam doors and shout. It'll take my mind off things." He took another measured mouthful. "Does she spend much time by the river?" he asked, keeping his voice casual.

Charlene's sharp glance told him she wasn't fooled. "Not anymore. She's always on her laptop or her phone."

"That's good to hear." Samuel felt another attack coming and put down his glass only just in time.

Charlene waited until he'd finished coughing. "Are you sure you don't need something...?"

"Bed, I think. It's been a long day."

Charlene sighed again, eyes deep wells of worry. "Good night, Samuel. Sleep well."

***

Somewhat to his surprise, Samuel did sleep well, deep and dreamless; and the first day went by relatively smoothly. Charlene had assigned him as his bedroom the downstairs den that had belonged to her husband; he spent a peaceful morning setting up his laptop and books. He sat before the window, with a mug of the herbal tea the doctor had recommended, while outside the shadows shifted on the lawn and the river glimmered through the trees.

He saw Lenora stalking about, eyeing him sidelong, and he guessed, whatever dire threats Charlene might have delivered, that it would not be long before she confronted him directly. Sure enough, that very first day, after Charlene had driven off to work, she marched right up, staring at him with laser eyes.

"Are you really sick?" she asked.

"If by 'sick,' you mean dying, then yes," Samuel said calmly, taking a sip of tea.

She recoiled. "Dying?"

"Yes. I've got about six months or so."

"Oh. I'm sorry." Lenora shifted awkwardly. "Is that why you came here?"

"More or less. I want to finish my book too."

She looked even more surprised at this. "Book?"

"Economic history of the northeast."

"Oh." Her face fell flat with boredom. "Well, uh, can I get you anything? Or do anything?"

"No, I'm fine. Though if you could avoid playing music really loudly, I'd appreciate it."

As he'd intended, she giggled at this, whole face brightening. "I promise." She checked her phone, suddenly adult. "I've got a babysitting job in a couple of hours anyway."

"Good luck with that. I hope they're not too awful."

Again, she laughed. "No, not too bad. But, seriously, is there anything I can do?"

Samuel smiled at her, sadly. "No, Lenora. Nothing."

***

The rest of the week passed quietly enough. But, that Saturday night, it rained.

Samuel had been watching the clouds gather all afternoon, dark and heavy with water, and as night fell, hastened by the clouds, the rain began to fall. Warm, heavy summer rain, beating down, bouncing off the leaves, billowing in sheets before the wind, soaking everything, hissing into the river. Samuel listened to the water gushing past, its sigh and roar.

Samuel and Charlene were both silent and uneasy, preoccupied with memories thirty years old. Lenora, picking up on the adults' mood, said nothing, but interrogated them with wide dark eyes.

Samuel answered none of her silent questions. Avoiding her gaze, he went to bed, alone in the thrashing, moaning night.

He woke up suddenly, past midnight. The night was silent, the storm passed on, but the doors were open. He could feel them in the sudden gulf of strangeness, hear them in the barely audible voices outside.

Slowly, Samuel stood up, pushing his feet into sneakers, and stepped out down the hall. The house was full of shadows; he moved silently through them and out into the rain-spangled yard.

The clouds had cleared, making way for the moon. Silver light sparkled everywhere, flashing from puddles and twinkling in the jewels lining the edges of leaves.

At the end of the yard, the river rushed, the moonlight dancing on its surface.

Samuel made his way to the bottom of the yard and sank down on the wooden bench, heedless of the wet. The bench had not been here, thirty years ago.

It had been so dark that night. And the rain had been so hard.

"Samuel."

Samuel looked down and was not at all surprised to see the dripping black head peering up at him from the water's edge, nor the long white arms braced against the bank. A thin face grinned at him, as pale as his own was dark. In the water, a silver tail flashed.

"Hello," he said wearily.

A sharp-toothed, green smile flashed. "Samuel. It is you. It's been long..." The siren pulled herself onto the bank, tail dissolving into legs as she crept closer. She sat down on the bench beside him, cold fingers crawling over Samuel's face and hands. "Thin," she mourned, her voice like water chattering over rocks. "So thin...You're dying."

"Yes," Samuel said, stiff and upright. "Yes, I am."

She let out a keen, bending over his hands, cold lips pressed against his flesh. "Poor Samuel...So young."

"I'm human. Humans die."

The siren stood up, pale breasts peeking from her curtain of hair. "Come, Samuel. You won't die." She nodded at the water.

Samuel looked at the river. Moonlight still frosted its black surface, but it was more restless than before, waves churning over its black depths. "No."

"She's there," said the siren. "She's still there. Beneath."

Samuel sat still by the black river, memories of a black river flickering. "Is she."

"Yes. Still there. Still there, Samuel. With us." The siren was flowing now, flesh transforming into water that trickled back over the bank. "You'll be with us. Pretty Samuel. Soon, Samuel. Sooooon..." Her voice slipped away as she dissolved, flowing over the bank and splashing back into the river.

Samuel sat a long moment before standing up and making his way back in the darkness.

***

It was difficult to concentrate the next day.

Samuel sat before his laptop as usual, but only occasionally tapped at the keys. Outside, the yard was still covered with raindrops, sparkling and refracting the fresh morning sunlight, while the river gushed beyond, strengthened by its dousing last night. Overhead, the trees dipped leafy branches into the water. It was a beautiful scene, but Samuel watched it through a haze of dark memories and steadily growing pain.

Behind him, the door opened and Lenora stood in the doorway, awkwardly balanced on one leg. "Hey. Uncle Samuel." She cut herself off abruptly.

"Yes, Lenora?" Outside, a bird swooped down for a bath in a puddle, splashing and cheeping.

"Uh...you need anything? From, like, the store? 'Cause Mom said to ask you."

Samuel shook his head. "No. Thank you, Lenora. I'm going to the doctor's tomorrow."

"Yeah." Lenora shifted to her other leg. "This must be really bad," she said at last.

"Well, I'd rather not die at the age of thirty-nine," Samuel agreed with a faint smile. "But we don't always get a choice about these things."

Lenora shifted yet again, and Samuel watched with interest and some amusement as curiosity welled up within her expression, warred with guilt and embarrassment, and won out.

"So, Uncle Samuel. What happened?"

"What happened when?" he asked, though he already knew.

"When you were kid. Mom won't talk about it. But didn't somebody die?"

"My twin sister," Samuel said shortly. "Her name was Arianne."

Lenora forgot even to wriggle in her sudden horror. "Oh, my God. What happened?"

"She drowned. We used to come here every summer, you see. Arianne liked playing by the river. One night she slipped and fell in."

"In the river?" Lenora was temporarily distracted by this new puzzle. "But how? That river's two feet deep, max!"

Images flashed: the churning waves that night, over the bottom-less black abyss, the depths that went down and down. "A person can drown in three inches of water," he said, "if they're facedown long enough."

"Oh. I'm sorry." Lenora looked ready to climb out of her skin with discomfort, but couldn't resist one last question. "How old was she?"

"We were nine." Nine years old and clinging to the rain-slick roots, freezing cold, while shining black heads emerged from the churning water, silver forms rising from the depths and those voices ringing through the rain, that chorus of unearthly voices from the black caves below.

"That's awful. I'm sorry."

Samuel shrugged. There was, in his experience, very little he could say to this.

"How could you come back here?" Lenora's eyes were wide. "If this is where she died?"

Samuel smiled a little. "That's why I came back, Lenora." And I hope you never have to understand that.

Lenora clearly did not. She shifted around some more. "Oh." Pause. "I'm really sorry, but...please don't tell Mom I asked, okay? She'll kill me."

Samuel grinned. "Your secret's safe with me."

"Thanks." Lenora paused; then asked, rather helplessly, "You need anything now? Tea? Medicine?"

Samuel decided to take mercy. "Some tea would be great, thanks," he said, and let her scamper off.

***

The rain might have passed, but there was a full moon that night.

It took a conjunction of circumstances for the doors to open; by itself, a full moon was not quite enough. No sirens would be crawling out of the water tonight, but there was no denying that a full summer moon on the sleek, rain-swollen river would thin the boundary, making the barrier shifty and uncertain.

Samuel dreamed.

He was nine years old again, skinny and shivering in the darkness of a rainy night, thin fingers clinging to the wet roots as Arianne, smiling dreamily, was pulled down by the multiple arms and eager faces, into the black river. Samuel cried out— Arianne!—and the sirens all turned, swishing around to gape in astonishment, eyes white and wide in the darkness.

Then he himself was journeying, swooping to the middle of the rain-pounded river. No sign of Arianne or her escorts now; but he dived down, the water striking him like a tearing veil as he entered the depths below.

Not the shallow pools that humans knew: those pebbly, sunlit shallows that could scarcely hide the trout that flashed from wading feet. No, these were the depths that lay behind the doors, that went down and down, past all light, past all laughter save that of the sirens as they flashed past him, black hair waving in the current, green teeth gleaming, escorting him further and further down, to their watery grottoes lit by phosphorescent algae, where Arianne waited.

Not the Arianne he had known and remembered still, but the creature she had become. Her arms long and graceful, glimmering with strings of shells and polished stones, round breasts blooming darkly among her cloud of black hair. Her silver tail shone, and her smile was as green and fanged as her sisters'.

She reached for him. Said his name.

And Samuel awoke.

He lay there a long time, alone in the moon-drunk night, and wondered if, even with the doors closed, the creatures that waited below the river could hear his pounding heart.

***

The next day, Charlene took him to the doctor, driving him out of town and past cow pastures and fields to the nearest hospital. It was a quiet drive through the hills, but not a particularly peaceful one. Still reeling from the dream, Samuel was unresponsive to Charlene's communicative sallies, and the medical inspection itself did not help matters.

"I think Dr. Lee's right," Charlene lectured as they made their way back to the car. "You need better care than this little place can provide!"

"We've been over this, Charlene," Samuel said wearily. He opened the door and threw in the latest prescription, still in its plastic bag. "All the care in the world won't do me much good now. And I want to die with some dignity, not hooked up to a bunch of machines."

Charlene glared at him, eyes bright and hard.

"What?" he demanded.

"Nothing," she said, and swung herself into the car.

Sighing, Samuel followed her.

As he'd expected, she turned to him almost immediately. "It's about Arianne, isn't it." It was not a question.

Samuel sat back in his baking-hot seat. "Yes. Yes, it is."

"It happened, Samuel." Her voice was firm. "She's with God now. And nothing's going to bring her back."

Samuel sat and stared at the sunlit windshield, at the heat-blistered parking lot beyond, and saw only dark water, cold shadows, and flashing silver scales. "What if she's not with God?"

"What?"

"What if she's still there?" Samuel spoke more strongly. "Still in the river?" He paused. "Beneath the river."

"Samuel." There was an edge of exasperation his cousin's voice now; and just a little fear. "I know what you thought you saw. But—you were nine years old—there's no such thing—"

Samuel thought of the siren, dissolving into river water at his feet. He thought of his dream. *I wish you were right, Charlene.* "Just keep Lenora away from that river, okay?"

After a moment, Charlene started the car.

***

When they got back, it was late afternoon and Lenora was not in the house.

She wasn't babysitting either, or shopping, or out with friends. She was sitting on the bench, staring out at the river.

Samuel, pausing halfway down the lawn to catch his breath, frowned at her. She had her smartphone, but it lay limp in her grasp; she wasn't texting, or reading, or listening to music. She simply sat and looked at the shifting shadows, deepening by the minute, broken by the dancing patches of light. He couldn't see her expression from where he stood, but there was something about her stillness, her silence, that was as familiar as it was disturbing.

Arianne. "Lenora," he said, before bending over another coughing attack.

Thank God, she turned her head immediately, and he saw the tranced look drain from her dark eyes. She stood up, hurrying over. "Uncle Samuel? Are you okay?"

"F-fine," he choked out. He peered at her worriedly. "Are you okay?"

"Me?" she blinked. "Yeah, I'm fine. Why?"

"You were...just sitting there. By the river. I didn't-didn't think you heard me."

"I...I..." For a moment, she looked lost, eyes wide as she groped for words. "I don't know; I just wanted to sit for a bit."

"How long were you there?" It came out sharper than he'd intended.

"I-I'm not sure. Lost track of time, I guess." She pushed back strands of dyed hair, distractedly. "Uh-how did the doctor's go?"

"About as expected. Lenora, what were you doing?"

"Nothing, okay! Just looking at the river. That a crime?"

"No, but—" He broke off, doubling over another coughing fit.

Lenora's face softened. "Come on, Uncle Samuel, let's go in..."

Samuel willingly let her lead him solicitously back into the house, relieved at every step that took them farther from the water, while knowing it was not far enough.

***

The moon waned, the days continued hot and clear, and the doors did not open; but Lenora grew more and more silent. She went through her days with a distracted air, barely responding to her mother's increasingly exasperated questions and demands, and there was no keeping her away from the river. More and more, she was to be found sitting on the bench, with or without her phone, staring hard at the water, fascinated by the shifts of light. The adults did their best to keep her away, calling her from the water's edge, but she was less and less responsive, her head always tilted, eyes slanted away.

"What's wrong with her?" Charlene demanded in frustration. "It's like she's always got her earphones in, even when she doesn't! What's she listening to?"

Samuel said nothing, but he knew exactly what she was listening to. Knew, because he could hear it too.

It was a far-off, dim sound by day: their voices just barely brushing the edge of his hearing, not quite audible, but always present. The eerie chorus grew louder at twilight, when blue dusk lay along the river; but it was during his sleep that Samuel heard them most clearly. And saw them.

It was not the knife-edged clarity of his full-moon vision, but still he saw: saw the caverns beneath the surface, darkly glimmering with ancient gold, and the sirens floating, their hair storms around their heads, their mouths open in the song. Arianne floated among them, tail beating the water lazily as she sang, her eyes shining as she looked up toward the surface. Toward Lenora. And toward him.

The sirens never forgot a human they desired. Especially not if that human had surprised them.

Samuel wasn't sure, but he suspected that Lenora was going out at night; the back door was always unlocked in the morning, and there were strange, muddy footprints on the floor. He always scrubbed them away before Charlene noticed; there was no point getting Lenora into trouble. He examined them as he wiped them away. Sometimes they were sneaker prints, but more often they were narrow bare feet, mixed with sand and blades of grass. Sometimes they were still wet come morning. There were dark circles now, under Lenora's eyes, and she was quieter than ever.

Samuel waited up one evening, avoiding the prescription sleeping pill, resisting the pull of exhaustion. It was the night of the dark of the moon and the song was dimmer tonight, the river's power less insistent, but he guessed that Lenora would still not be able to resist, and he was right.

He heard her sneaking quietly down, pausing before venturing across the floor, slowly easing the back door open. The dim sound of her footsteps across the porch, then silence as she descended onto the lawn.

Samuel waited a long moment before levering himself out of bed.

He was getting weaker now; his heart pounded as he stumbled and shuffled down the hall and out the door. Outside, the night was still, so bright with stars that, even without the moon, a grayish twilight filled the yard. But the shadows were black cutouts, and the river sang invisible in the darkness beneath the trees.

Down at the river's edge, a splash.

Samuel made his way down the lawn. "Hey."

He could just barely make out her shadowy form, feet dangling in the water. "Uncle Samuel...?"

"Can you hear them?" With great effort, Samuel lowered himself to the ground beside her.

"Yeah." She pulled her feet out of the water with a splashing gush. "They're not so loud tonight."

"There's no moon. Moonless nights strengthen the barrier. Moonlight opens it, a little. But, really, summer rain is best."

Lenora hummed a little, swaying beside him. "I hear them all the time."

"They're singing to you. The way they sang to Arianne."

She stopped. "Arianne?"

"You think she drowned?" Samuel laughed mirthlessly. "I was there. I saw them pull her down."

"Down where?"

"Below the river."

"The river?"

"Below it. There are places...caves that exist beneath the river—
or maybe somewhere else and the river's only the door to them,
I don't know. They live there. In the deep caves, full of water.
They live there, and they watch us, but they can only rise when
the conditions are right. Like when there's a summer rainstorm,
at night."

"Like that night?"

"Precisely. They sang to Arianne, like they're singing to you, and
she went out to them, during that rainstorm, and they pulled her
down, and now she's one of them."

"What are they?" Her voice was fascinated, soft in the night.

"I call them the sirens, but I don't know what their proper name
is. If anyone knows...They're the ones beneath the river. They're
immortal, always young, always beautiful, but they're dangerous. They take humans. Girls, women who can see them."

"You saw them."

"I'm maybe the only man who ever did. They were so surprised,
that I could see them..." He remembered their astonishment:
their wide eyes, their shocked face turning in the water as he
cried out: Let her go! Those long arms grabbing for him... "I
escaped. But they never forgot me."

"Why'd you come back, then?" Lenora's voice held only interest
and curiosity; she was, perhaps, too siren-spelled to feel any fear,
even now. "If you knew they'd be here."

"Because...I was sick..." But it was too late for lies, even to himself. "Because it was inevitable."

There was a moment's silence, broken only by the soft, continuing song.

"You know, I'm probably not going to believe any of this in the morning," Lenora said eventually.

"Daylight has that effect," said Samuel. "But day always ends. And there's always another moon." Slowly, effortfully, he pulled himself to his feet. "Come on; let's go in."

"I want to stay here..."

"Lenora."

With a sigh, she stood up and trailed off up the lawn, casting glances behind at the river.

Samuel stayed behind, like a sentinel by the dark flow, and it wasn't until the door safely slammed behind Lenora that he followed her in.

***

The next day dawned, but Lenora was worse than ever.

"For God's sake, Lenora, eat your breakfast!" yelled Charlene, covering her fear with anger. Lenora looked languidly away from the window to spoon up more cereal, still staring into the distance.

As Samuel shuffled by, Charlene paused in her harried going—to—work preparations to nod at Lenora. "Keep an eye on her, okay? Make sure she eats."

"You've got to get her away from that river," he muttered back. Lenora was staring out the window again, meal forgotten.

"How?" Charlene demanded, with an edge of hysteria. "I can't take time off work!"

"Then arrange for her to get a job out of town. Or I'll pay for her to go to summer camp. Or something."

"I'll think about it," said Charlene, which was, Samuel knew, the closest she was going to get to admitting that he was right. "And eat your breakfast!" she snapped again at Lenora before whirling out.

Samuel sat down at the table. Lenora barely responded to his arrival, head tilted as she listened to the music.

"You know, I think I do believe you," she said abruptly. "Even now."

"The sirens are hard to ignore," he agreed.

She hummed, smiling dreamily as she swayed to the sirens' tune. "It's so beautiful…"

"It is that." Samuel looked outside. The light was grayish; the day heavy with humidity. He couldn't see it from here, but he imagined that the sky was starting to gather clouds. "Not long now, until it rains."

Lenora looked up at this, half-hopeful, half-afraid. "Will we see them then?"

"I hope not," Samuel said. But he didn't think his hope would be fulfilled.

The pair sat at the kitchen table, listening to the sirens.

***

The day grew ever more oppressive, dark and humid; and the days that followed were worse. The clouds mounted in the sky, the air grew still and breathless, and still it did not rain.

Lenora's babysitting jobs were suspended; the neighbors thought—not incorrectly—that she was ill. Charlene, seeming to heed Samuel's words, gave her lists of things to do, that took her out of the house, and Samuel did his best to steer her away from the river's edge. Still, she spent long hours sitting by it, gazing at its flow and listening. Truth be told, so did Samuel. It was getting ever more difficult to ignore the sirens' call; it was easier just to sit and let the music flow.

"What's it like down there?" Lenora asked suddenly on the afternoon of the third day. Overhead, the clouds were like a low gray lid.

"I'm not sure," said Samuel; and paused to catch his breath. It was getting harder to speak, harder to walk. He could barely make it down the lawn now. "Only what...I've seen in dreams. It's dark but t...beautiful. The caves are beautiful. There's glowing algae, and flashing fish, and treasures older than...than the human race." He broke off, silenced by a coughing attack. "But there's no warmth. No light. No love."

Lenora put out a steadying hand, but her gaze remained on the river. "Doesn't Arianne still love you?"

Samuel pulled in a deep, rasping breath. "I don't know," he said hoarsely. "I honestly don't know."

There was a sudden, warm impact on his hand. Samuel looked at the drop of water; then glanced up to see the next few drops splashing into the river.

Lenora held up a hand, gathering raindrops as they increased momentum. "It's raining."

"So it is."

Lenora had to help him to his feet before they went in, while all around them the rainstorm slowly gathered strength.

***

Samuel was not sure what woke him that night.

It might have been the rain, pounding harder than ever on his window. It might have been the siren song, increasing its volume. It might have been Lenora, walking past his room. Or maybe it was just the doors, slowly opening between the depths and the surface...

Samuel got up. Though the song was pounding in his brain, flowing through his soul, his body's weakness made him slow. He moved like one in a drug-laced dream as he shuffled, barefoot, out of his room and down the hall.

Lenora had not closed the door behind her, and the scents and sounds of the night flowed in: rain, wind, grass and leaves, all sighing and gusting in the storm. But through it all, the sirens sang, their voices all the louder for the tempest.

"Lenora," Samuel called, but his voice was so weak now he could barely raise it above a whisper. Cursing his pain and exhaustion, he stumbled out into the night.

He was soaked in instants, the tree branches shaking and screaming above him. Lashed by the winds, his pajamas whipping against his legs, he hobbled down the lawn, where he could just barely make out Lenora's thin still form by the churning water. "Lenora!"

But she had already stepped off the edge, into the sirens' embrace.

Arms wrapped around her, heads leaning in, eager-like last time, like thirty years ago—their voices raised in wild laughter, their tails foaming the rocking water: deep, deep water that reached down to the bottom of the world, to the caves that preceded earthly existence. The river that was not the river frothed with whitecaps, and Samuel saw Arianne's daggered green smile as she pulled their cousin down—

"Wait."

His voice was a mere puff of air in the rain-mad tempest, but still they heard him, all their wet heads turning. In their grasp, Lenora stirred, languidly, and gave a dreamy giggle.

Arianne unwound her arms and broke away, surging through the waves to the bank. She hauled herself out, her legs growing from her tail. A moment's unbalance, and then she stood before her brother, eyes bright, smile beaming.

"Samuel," she sighed, her voice the rain on the river.

"Arianne," he replied, with a sigh of his own.

Her eyes devoured him, blackly glowing in the night. "It's been so long."

"Thirty years," Samuel said. "It's good to see you again, Arianne."

She laughed, briefly. "And you."

"Don't take her, Arianne." Samuel gestured toward Lenora's prone figure, still held at the surface by the still, listening sirens. "She's not the one you really want. You know that. Take me instead."

Arianne considered him gravely. "You'll come with us?"

"Yes. Leave Lenora here—leave her alone—and I'll come with you."

Slowly, a beautiful smile grew on Arianne's face, until even her hair was shining with her joy. She held out her long arms, gleaming with shells and stones.

Without hesitation, Samuel stepped into her embrace. It was cold and tight and hard, but still, there was peace there, and relief. For, at last, the struggle was over.

"Samuel," his sister sighed, "you're home."

***

Lenora was drowning.

She cried out, kicking against the freezing, frenzied water-was this the river?—as the arms that had supported her unwound, letting her fall away. She went under, the waves sucking at her, pulled herself to the surface, gasped for air. Her kicking legs touched nothing but water: she could feel the infinite depths below her.

Then cold-clawed hands grabbed her, pulled her, hauled her roughly through the water. Lenora was pulled down, came up gasping, but still the hands yanked her on. Unceremoniously, the siren shoved her out onto the muddy bank, turning back without a second glance.

Desperately, Lenora grabbed at the slippery roots, hauling herself up, rolling out onto the grass. Sobbing, she lay, beaten by the rain, face and clothes smeared with mud, and looked out at the river.

The water heaved, but still the sirens gathered, untroubled by the waves, around another prone figure, held at the surface in their multiple supporting arms. It was Samuel, Lenora saw, who lay among the creatures, his face serene in their black glow, the years seeming to fall away even as Lenora watched, the sharp light already entering his eyes, teeth turning green—

"No!" Lenora screamed, scrabbling forward, plunging back into the water, but already the sirens were pulling him down, their song crooning and loving as they retreated back below the surface.

And then Lenora stood, bedraggled and alone, in surging shallows that barely reached her knees, while the rain hissed into the empty river.

The Salt Debt

J.B. Rockwell

J.B. Rockwell writes speculative
fiction and anything else that
catches her fancy. Her adult sci-fi
series, SERENGETI, is available
from Severed Press.

Nana Moira sat in a corner, darning Socks by the fire. Silvered needles whipping and stitching, bony fingers steady and sure—certain as any surgeon's hand.

"Silly puss lost 'is head again," she cackled, tugging at the long, dark thread.

An old joke, that one, and much reused, just like everything in that tiny stone and thatch cottage. But Daidoe Seamus laughed anyway, just as he always did. A sharp sound of creaking springs and crab claws clacking, the brass key driving his long-dead heart turning slow circles as it jutted from his chest.

I watched those two together as I floated languidly in my bath. Measured the love that flowed between them—tangible as the scents of liniment and lavender hanging heavy on the air. And I, being granddaughter and dutiful, laughed with them. My own voice a blubbering bubble rising upward from the brining vat in which my tentacled body reposed.

A song of yearning. Of envy most foul.

No clockworks for me, after all. The sea claimed my body, spitting back just my head, but Nana Moira worked a deal with yon Alders Bay Kraken. Offering the Great Beast a gift of life eternal—a clockwork framework of brass and gold—in exchange for a single seed. Nana Moira's pick of the litter from the Kraken's next get.

Death begot death and from it life. A short one for me—just a hundred years and five before this Kraken's body came apart—but long enough, really. Enough years to suit me, who'd died once already and drifted downward in the salty dark.

A last loving cackle, one more whipping stitch, and Nana Moira tied off a snug knot, right under Socks' black and white chin. Leaned in close, wrinkled lips disappearing in the patched and faded fur of Socks' patched and faded neck. Teeth nipping daintily as she expertly snapped the thread.

"There ya are, luv. Good as new." She chortled fondly, patting the old cat fondly on the rough fur of his snaggle-toothed head. Scooped his bag of bones body from her bag of bones lap and nuzzled her grey-skinned nose to his.

Daidoe Seamus watched her, saying not a word—not in all that time. Nor I either, lacking lungs of sufficient to drive the muscles of my larynx. I just thrashed my suckered legs in the briny sea bath I called home, whipping the water into a froth, spraying rainbow shimmer bubbles in the fire lit air.

Socks caught sight of one and batted at it lackadaisically, swiping with a nubbin clawed foot until the bubble drifted away, bursting brightly in the fire. He mewled mournfully, missing his catspaw already. Mewled again, rusted voice croaking as he swiped his worn, sandpaper tongue across the seamed landscape of Nana Moira's much wrinkled face.

"That's my boy," Nana Moira crooned. "That's my sweet prince."

A peck on the nose and Nana Moira set Socks on the floor, steadying his bony old body with her knob-knuckled fingers as he tottered over to the knitting basket. An oversized whicker seashell overflowing with yarn bundles, strategically placed between the tickling reach of Nana Moira's fingers and the decadent warmth of the crackling fire.

I flicked a stream of water at him as Socks settled down, salted droplets sparkling as they dusted the air, raining down like diamonds on his onyx and snow fur.

Socks barely noticed—an old game, this one, like Nana Moira's jokes and cackling laughter—and he an old puss. Ancient, by feline standards at nine and ninety years. Wise as the broad-winged owl who sheltered in Nana Moira's barn, and grown accustomed to his comforts.

The soft food Nana Moira fed him, and the touch of her gentle, skilled fingers. The warmth of the glowing fire, the occasional fat mouse with which to amuse himself. Socks mounted his throne of yarn with stiff-legged steps and settled into a softly carved out nest. A lick at his tail-thin and worn like all the rest of him—and he erupted with purr, clockworks ticking like castanets inside his belly and chest.

Nana Moira touched at him, and at her temple, her own emaciated breast. Storm grey eyes looking sad now, wrinkled face—once so beautiful, now an aged, sage roadmap one and thirty and one years in the making—turning thoughtful. Filling with regret.

"Seamus," she said, soft voice flowing like honey. Like all the love in the world. "Seamus, luv, it's time."

Daidoe Seamus looked at me, freckled hand lifting to turn the key embedded in his chest. A sigh escaped him—dry as dust, a sound of aspen leaves fluttering in a winter wind—as he stepped close to Nana Moira's chair, knelt down and took her head between his hands.

Stroked her cheek as the light in her eyes dimmed, and her

heart—overburdened by one hundred and thirty and one years of love and learning and infinite patience—slowed its beating. Thumped once and stopped.

Socks yowled pitifully from his woolen string lair. Daidoe Seamus yowled with him—a groaning, moaning, grief—filled wail of despair.

And I...I was dutiful. I was granddaughter and the last of our line. Witness to Nana Moira's last breath.

Helpless. Useless. Just like when Mama passed.

Not this time, I decided. Not again.

Daidoe Seamus bowed his head in mourning, clockworks ticking endlessly inside his chest, as I took up Nana Moira's needles—stretching to take them from her hand. Balanced those silvered spears with exhausting exactness, holding them carefully in my tentacle hands.

Steeled myself as I drove the points downward, piercing one Kraken leg and another, black blood spurting in fountains, turning green as ichor, as poison most foul. Swirled in snaking patterns, mixing with the oily brine of my bath.

A last sharp-tipped puncture and I dragged myself from the salt soup that sustained me, flopped to the floor and tentacle-walked to the corner and Nana Moira's chair. Conscious of Socks watching me, golden eyes shining with fire. Of Daidoe Seamus cranking his heart-shaped key, priming the heart-shaped organ sitting inside his chest.

He stood, kissing Nana Moira's cooling hand before backing away, standing betwixt Socks and the fire's flames. The two of them bearing mute witness as I, in the firelight, scaled the wooden frame of Nana Moira's perch. Clutched at her woolens to hug her to me and splay my tentacled body across her chest.

Held her tightly, like a lover in the night. Sobbing softly as I reached for the last of Nana Moira's workings, gathering the trailing end of yarn dangling from her limp, dead hand. A touch at her cheek to inject the poison and I slowly, painstakingly rebuilt the patterns. Knitting myself to her. Creating a replacement for Nana Moira's stone dead heart.

The Joy of Baking

Holly Lyn Walrath

Holly Lyn Walrath is a writer of
poetry and short fiction. Her work
has appeared in Strange Horizons,
The Fem, and Crab Fat Magazine,
and her poetry was nominated
for the SFPA Rhysling Award.
She is a freelance editor, contract
editor with Writership.com,
and volunteer with Writespace,
a nonprofit literary center in
Houston, Texas. She currently
resides in Seabrook, Texas. Find
her online @hollylynwalrath or
hlwalrath.com

It's amazing how much easier it is to bake a cake when you've got an eternity to get it right. The secret to effective baking is patience, followed by the ability to fold the batter with a metal spoon instead of rushing in with a wooden spoon like a hammer. The folding in must be gentle so as not to break the hard-earned bubbles of air. Lastly, a baker must have the willingness to guard the oven, your feet cold on the tile, letting the warm scents of butter and vanilla envelop you and seep into the whole house, holding your breath while the batter rises, goldens, and browns slightly at the edges.

Timing is everything.

***

"Not quite perfect, but deliciously close," Luciana proclaims as she places the angel food into her mouth and tastes the air-soft sweetness, the tart explosion of raspberry on her tongue. She takes one red berry and parses each bulb from its partners, rolls it in her mouth.

"What do you think?" Sofia asks their guests. The souls at the table nibble at their cakes but do not speak.

"They're too new to answer, Sofia, you know that," Luciana chides. She flits around the table, piping more whipped cream onto each plate in little rosettes.

"I know. It just feels somehow impolite not to ask." Sofia stands and carries another slice to the last soul at the table. A thin manifestation of what was once a thin man. He still wears the jaundice of the alcoholism that brought him to their table. Watching Sofia warily, he eats the cake with his hands. She pushes the fork towards him with gentle eyes, but he ignores her, shredding the cake into pieces that slip away like pilfered coins. He's eating to fill a void, but Sofia can tell he doesn't like the cake by the downward turn of his mouth.

Sofia and Luciana are very good at baking cakes. They've made thousands, perhaps millions of cakes, but who's counting? Being immortal, the constraints of time simply don't concern them.

Six new souls sit at the table today. It's a big wooden table, painted white, with sturdy chairs wearing knitted cushions. The house is furnished for comfort, farm-like, although there aren't any animals, aren't any fields of corn out beyond the porch. The kitchen is large and airy. Its cabinets are white with wood curlicues carved onto the handles. A modern, or at least modern to them, oven stands on one side. There's also an old-fashioned wood stove they sometimes roast marshmallows in.

Outside, galaxies pass by in the window over the sink. The flare of a dying world is almost like a sunset, the dusk of a nebula almost like a summer thunderstorm, the billion stars gleaming in the night almost like real stars. Almost.

Sofia and Luciana clear the table and then help the souls upstairs into garret rooms with wood beam ceilings, and guest rooms with neat white furniture, and side rooms with beds tucked between bookcases filled with more books than they could ever read.

The souls will sleep, rest from the shock of transference, and then move along when they are ready to venture into their next body. This is an in-between place. A space between lives.

***

"I smell cake again," Hiran announces, watching Luciana shuffle the jaundiced man into one of the bedrooms. The man closes the door in her face.

Luciana is pleased to note Hiran's gained weight. His soul displays signs of permanence now. His former body, that of an emaciated eight-year-old boy, is now healthy and robust. The curve of his cheek is harder, his dark eyes more distinct, and Luciana sees brightness in their depths now, along with intelligence tempered by humor. Hiran is less transparent, more real-looking in his solidity. When he reaches full embodiment he will depart this former shell, leave Luciana and Sofia, and move on. But for now, Luciana revels in his little boy impatience, his funny jokes and gentle kindness to the other souls. She knows her role in this place, just as each ingredient in a cake has its role to play: proteins bonding with flour to create gluten, eggs making sure the mixture holds together, baking powder and baking soda releasing carbon dioxide to help the batter rise.

"Come get a slice then, before it's gone," Luciana says, and tweaks his ear.

"Ow," Hiran protests, although it doesn't hurt. "Okay." He follows her back to the table and eats his cake slice in two gulping bites. "Let's play a game."

"Okay, what game shall we play?"

Hiran pauses to think. "What about Carrom?"

"Again?" Luciana teases, retrieving the game from the closet, which is chock-full of every board game imaginable, from nearly every culture. The house provides what they want. They only need think of it and it appears.

As Luciana and Hiran trade strikes Sofia walks back into the kitchen. "The crying man passed on. I gave him his hat and sent him on his way," she says.

"Good," Luciana says. "It was time." It's been many years since Luciana felt the need to escort every soul on. She now knows some people go better alone, and others prefer her or Sofia only. She pockets a man with a smile at Hiran, who sighs.

"You're too good at this game," he moans, and Luciana and Sofia laugh because he always picks the same game to play. "If you called Joshua 'the crying man', what do you call me?"

"We call you boy who eats all the cake!" Sofia says, noting the empty metal tin on the table.

Hiran hides his pleasure, like most boys of his age do with older women. "You'll make more tomorrow."

"This is true," Sofia says. "We probably will."

***

Cake is universal. Everyone likes a certain kind of cake, even those who claim not to like it at all. Sofia's found the right cake for most every soul that enters their home, although some go too quickly to enjoy it. Some linger, clinging to the last life, unable to settle the worries of what they left behind. Others revel in cake, never able or allowed to eat it in life.

Sofia lies awake before sleep and listens to Luciana's breathing next to her. It's a sound she's memorized like the sound of tres leches sizzling in the oven. It was her favorite cake as a child. All the things she wanted in her past are hers now. At first she worried not growing old might be hard, that she might regret not bearing a child, but she doesn't feel that way anymore. She used to think she'd miss Death, her erstwhile lover, but she can hardly remember the smell of his skin. Those were the wants of another Sofia in another world. That Sofia didn't know how to bake, didn't know how to show kindness, and didn't know how to love. This Sofia treats each day as new and never rushes the air out of the batter, knowing so much of the tender, melt-in-the-mouth sweetness of cake comes from space and time.

***

The jaundiced soul doesn't like angel food cake. He doesn't like tres leches, apple bottom, birthday, turtle, pumpkin chiffon, cheesecake, or cookie cake. He perks up momentarily on the day Sofia and Luciana make chocolate rum raisin cake, but Sofia suspects it's just the rum.

His words are on her in the kitchen before she allows herself to sense his presence. "How did you get this job anyway?"

Sofia falters as the scent of rum fills the kitchen. She stirs the raisins until they melt down to sugary glory. The hesitation is a holdover from her old life, but she relents. This man won't remember this story after he's gone. "I fell in love with Death."

"The guy with the scythe?"

"Well, he doesn't carry a weapon anymore, but yes. I met him when he came for my mother. I traveled with him for a few years. Then he needed an assistant so I signed on to do this work. And that's how I met Luciana." Sofia waves a wooden spoon in Luciana's direction and Luciana winks over the batter.

"The work of baking for dead people?" The man asks.

"No, that's just a perk of the job."

The man tries to poke a finger in the rum mixture but nothing happens.

"It doesn't come into being until it gets baked in the oven," Sofia explains.

The rum bottle goes missing that day. Sofia finds it on the porch but doesn't have the heart to tell the man alcohol doesn't have the same properties here. He won't tell them his name. His soul stays as glass-thin as the day he arrived. His skin is streaked with the threads of addiction like cinnamon in swirls. His head is shaved down to nicks and cuts but stubble is heavy on his chin. He wears a tattered shirt. His fingers are cigarette-black, his teeth yellow. His once-beautiful blue eyes shimmer with disgust.

***

"Do you think we bother him?" Luciana wonders aloud to Sofia, as they prepare a German chocolate cake. Luciana's face is pink with the effort of beating the egg whites by hand with a metal whisk. After grating coconut and chopping pecans, Sofia rubs her hands together to distribute them in the icing. It's happened before—but usually souls only fear them for a few days before realizing the conventions of their former society, whether they be about women or lovers, don't apply here. The only law is the one outside their doors.

"No," Sofia says. "He's still clinging to his former life. He needs more time."

He's already stayed the longest of any soul yet. They don't say this out loud. They aren't gatekeepers. It's not their job to judge;

this isn't really a job. They are feeders of the weary, their house a waystation for ways they themselves will never travel again.

Hiran comes running into the kitchen laughing. "Look, Sofia, Luciana, look!" he cries.

They look. He's reached full embodiment. He holds his fingers up to the light, marveling at their texture, their warmth, their realness. "Good boy." Luciana hugs him. For a moment his embrace feels as tangible to her as her own body, as real as any boy. She memorizes the feeling of his warmth, folding it into herself to keep for another day.

Sofia places a hand on Luciana's shoulder. "It's time then." Sofia and Luciana walk with Hiran to the back door. The jaundiced man is sitting on the couch, and he watches them open the door.

"What's out there?" Hiran wonders aloud.

"A new life. Perhaps a better one," Luciana says. She whispers a small prayer, a hope Hiran's next life will be better than the last, that he will be born to a loving parent who holds him close and perhaps bakes him cake.

Sofia bundles Hiran in a warm jacket despite his protests. "It might be cold where you're going." She doesn't know if this is true, but it feels right. Hiran complains the coat is too big, but he doesn't remove it.

On the porch, they watch the house float by nebulas, moons, stars, planets. A comet streaks through space like the flash of a knife in dough.

"Will I remember you?" Hiran asks at the last moment.

Luciana smiles. "No, dear. But that's alright."

Hiran gives them each a quick hug, his face red with little boy embarrassment at the show of affection. He waves, then steps off the porch steps. He disappears into the next world like fruit plunked into batter.

Sofia takes Luciana's hand in hers and squeezes it.

The jaundiced man steps past them. He reaches into the air where Hiran stood, but a slim barrier stops his fingers—invisible glass. "That's all it takes to get back?" His voice is incredulous.

"He's not gone back, he's gone forward," Sofia says.

"Why am I still here?"

"You have to let go," Luciana says.

"A lot of bad things happened to me." The jaundiced man scratches at transparent skin pockmarked with self-destruction. Years of self-loathing and habitual greediness shine on his body, just beneath the surface.

"That doesn't matter anymore," Sofia says.

"A lot of people deserve to pay for the things they did."

"You won't see them ever again," Luciana says.

"If I go on," the man pauses. He curls his fingers around the porch railing. "I'll forget my daughter. I owed her more than dying in a stinking puddle of my own piss like an old man."

Sofia sighs. "She won't know that. You're dead to her."

Luciana gives Sofia a look. Things are different for Luciana, who learned baking at the apron-strings of her mother so many years ago. "We can send her a message if you like. We can't guarantee she'll get it, but we can still try." Sofia tuts at her.

"Will it help?" He asks, looking Sofia in the eyes, as if he knows she is the more practical one, as if he knows Sofia was called first to this work, choosing immortality over life. Eternity with Luciana over Death, both the man and the next life.

Sofia says, "For you, maybe."

***

So he writes a letter to his daughter.

I'm sorry, the letter begins. *I did bad things. I should've been better, for you. You should do better, for you. And a lot of other things*, he explains. *The drinking, the women I thought I loved, the family I destroyed. I hope you go make it to college. I hope you get married one day. I love you*, he ends the letter, and it's the truth.

Luciana and Sofia roll the letter into a scroll like a brandy snap. They slide it into a soda bottle. The jaundiced man stands on the porch and flings it as far into space as he can.

"A part of my heart is in that bottle," he says. "The human leftovers, I guess."

"You'll be human again," Sofia replies.

Later, when the man eats the German chocolate cake, he cries and laughs. Sometimes cake does this to people. A certain flavor can bring back a thousand memories, a certain smell can awaken a million dreams. As he eats, Sofia thinks she can see him a little more clearly.

"I haven't eaten this in years," he says to Sofia and Luciana. "My gran used to make it."

Sofia smiles. She opens her recipe book as Luciana goes to the front door, where someone is knocking to be let in.

Flowers for the Moon

Clio Yun-Su Davis

Clio Yun-su Davis is a game designer and writer who splits her time between DC, New York City, and Austin, Texas. She studied interactive storytelling in the Interactive Telecommunications Program at NYU's Tisch School of the Arts, a graduate program she likes to describe as "sci-fi Hogwarts." When not writing fiction or creating games, she can usually be found working on an immersive theater project or living one of a thousand possible lives in a larp.

There once was a girl who fell in love with the moon even though she knew in her heart that the moon could never love her back, for it lived in the sky surrounded by thousands of stars that shone far more brightly than any mortal could. Just the same, when night fell she would step outside and gaze at the object of her affection in awe, wondering if it ever looked down and longed for her as she longed for it. So consumed was she by her infatuation that she did not notice the rest of the world as it moved and changed around her. To her the sun was worthless, the earth beneath her a burden, and the words of her family and friends little more than empty sounds to be forgotten as soon as they were carried off by the wind.

One day her mother grew so worried for her that she traveled to the outskirts of the town and brought back with her the crone who was once said to have been a prophetess for the Empress herself. The crone waited for the sun to fall–for the girl slept throughout most of the day–and then met with the lovelorn child as the insects sang in the light of her precious moon.

"Why is it that you have fallen in love with one so unattainable?" the crone asked her.

"Because I was lost in the dark one night in winter, and no one realized I was gone so no one thought to look for me. Just as I was about to give up hope and consign myself to dying in the cold, the clouds parted and there the moon was, shining down to reveal the path ahead."

The crone shook her head, the beads in her hair clicking against each other as she did. "Do you really believe it showed itself just for you? The moon illuminates everyone and everything. It sees more than you or I could ever imagine. Do you really think that it saw you and thought to reach out its light for you alone that night?"

The girl was quiet, her eyes downcast as she contemplated her answer.

"At first I was convinced that it did. But now I am not as sure. All I am certain of is that it saved me, whether it knows it or not. And I would very much like for it to know."

With a heavy but unsurprised sigh, the crone brought herself to her feet.

"Very well. Then there is only one thing to do. I will draw you a map."

The girl followed the crone outside, where the old woman grabbed her hand and dug a long, sharp fingernail into the girl's palm until four droplets of blood dripped down her arm. The first drop trailed all the way down to the bottom of her forearm, where it blossomed into a map of an emerald forest. The second drop landed above the first, and expanded to reveal an ocean of midnight blue, dotted with gray islands. The third drop fell only to her wrist, and unfurled into a vast desert of red rock that ended in a tall cliff that stretched high up into the sky.

The fourth drop remained in the girl's palm, where it formed a perfect picture of the white moon, surrounded by its stars. A line, bent and crooked in places, ran from the bottom of the forest all the way to the heavens.

"This path will first take you to a cave out at sea where you will find flowers the color of the kind of fire that only burns at the center of the earth. These will make a fine gift to your beloved moon as it has never seen such a thing before, even though its life has been such a long one. The path will then lead you to the one place where the moon is certain to see you–a desert where nothing grows, and the glow of your flowers will be sure to capture its attention. The rest is up to you."

The girl thanked the crone, unaware as she turned to walk towards the forest that the old woman was shaking her head in sorrow and pity.

"Another fool for love marches off into the darkness without so much as looking back," she said, and began her own trek back to her house at the edge of town.

***

The forest was dense, and as the girl walked, more and more of the sky–and the light of the moon–was blocked out by the leaves above. Though the girl was lonely without her moon, she knew she certainly was not alone. Strange sounds came from the dark spaces between the trees, and every once in a while what little light there was would be reflected in a pair of eyes so briefly that the girl had to wonder whether she really saw them at all.

Though the path marked on the map on her arm led her only deeper into the part of the forest that was filled with gnarled roots and low tangled branches, the girl did not stray from it. Eventually, however, it grew too dark to move forward, and she found a large tree to rest her back against as she closed her eyes for a bit. Without the moon and enshrouded by the blackness of night, fear filled the girl's heart, but she bit her lip and refused to give into it.

"Why have you come here?" someone asked, and the girl's eyes shot open but found no one there.

"I am on my way to the ocean," she answered, though she knew not to whom she spoke.

"And what do you plan to do when you reach it?" the voice asked.

"Travel across it to the desert."

"And once you are there?"

"I don't see why I should tell you that when I do not even know who you are."

The voice laughed, and as it did the branches above her head shook and the ground trembled.

"I am the forest that you have invaded. You carry my image upon your arm. The last time you were here there was snow on the ground and you were so frightened you could not hear me calling out to guide you."

The girl thought about this and wondered if it could be true. She did not remember hearing a voice when she was lost, but her ears had been full with the sound of her heartbeat as she weaved through the trees in panic.

"It was the moon who ended up saving me," she told the forest.

"How lucky you are, then," the forest replied in a tone she did not altogether appreciate.

"In fact, the reason I am heading to the desert is to confess my love for the moon."

"You are going to confess your love for the moon to the desert? Are you certain that the desert will care to hear that?"

"No, to the moon! I am going to confess to the moon!" the girl shouted, and the forest shushed her with the rustling of its leaves.

"You will wake up my fauna if you continue to make such a racket," the forest scolded her. "Now, why would you want to go and confess your love for something so distant as the moon? What, pray tell, is it that you are expecting to happen when you do so?"

"I suppose I want to know whether it loves me too."

"And if it does?" the forest asked.

"I don't know! Why do you ask so many questions of me?"

"Why do you not ask them of yourself?" said the forest. "They are important questions."

The girl was silent, for she knew despite her annoyance that the forest was right.

"I will think about it on my way there," the girl said with a sigh.

"And I will help you find your way to the ocean," said the forest.

***

When the sun rose and the girl could see, she set out again with the forest as her companion. Now that she could see more of it, she realized that the forest was really very beautiful. What was frightening at night was now serene, and instead of threatening eyes she saw curious rodents and shy foxes scurrying around in the underbrush. Where shadows once fell, flowers and moss were now visible, and the songs of dozens of birds surrounded her. As she moved through the forest she spoke with it and it told her wistfully about a time before humans, and when she reached its final trees she was almost sad to leave it behind.

"One piece of advice," the forest said as the girl stepped beyond its threshold. "The moon is lovely, but it is not the world. Choose wisely what you are willing to give up."

The girl did not think she understood fully what it was the forest meant, but she soon put it out of her mind when her feet reached the shore of the wide ocean and she was face to face with a boat she did not know how to sail. Once out at sea, it did not take long for her to stray from the path marked on her arm, for she could not get the boat to do what she wanted and soon she was curled up on the floor, sick from the rocking of the vessel.

"Forgive me if I am mistaken, but I do not believe this boat belongs to you," a voice said, but the girl was too ill to look for where it had come from.

"I did not see an owner, but I was in sore need," she replied.

"And now you are paying the price, for this boat does not obey anyone but its mistress, and you are not her."

"Please, how can I make it listen to me?" the girl asked.

"Well, I could have a word with it, but first I'd like to know why it is that you have stolen it," said the voice.

"I am on my way to pick flowers for the moon and confess my love to it."

The boat continued to rock back and forth in silence for a

moment, then finally it calmed itself. When the girl steered, it now obeyed, and soon they were back on their path towards the cave where the flowers grew.

"Thank you, whoever you are...and wherever you are," the girl said to the air around her, for she knew not to whom she spoke.

"Raise your eyes and you cannot miss me. I am the ocean, and I am very curious as to how you came to fall in love with the moon."

The girl told the ocean her story, and when it breathed a deep sigh, the boat tilted on its starboard side.

"Yes, I remember when I too first fell in love with the moon. To this day I still let it sway me, though we do not speak quite so often as we used to."

The girl had not considered before that something as great as the ocean might be at risk of feeling heartache, but as they talked on through the dawn, she came to understand that they shared a great deal, including that unique pain and joy that came with loving the moon.

When the boat came to rest on the shore of the small island marked on her arm, the girl hurried into the darkness of the cave, eager to find the flowers that the crone had instructed her to gift to her beloved. In the damp chill and surrounded by jagged rocks, the flowers grew and glowed so bright that they cast shadows on the walls. Though they were hot to the touch, the girl plucked them from the ground until they overflowed from her hand. The petals singed her fingers, but she wore a smile on her face as she returned to the boat triumphant.

When at last the ocean brought the girl and her flowers to the shore beyond which lay the desert, the girl was sad to part with its company. The ocean wished her luck, and she was on her way, the flowers burning in her grip.

It was not the heat of the sun that bothered her as the girl traversed the red wastes, nor the roughness of the rocks beneath her feet. It was the absence of life and the silence that accompanied it. Only the wind stirred out there in the emptiness, and without any sign of the cliff she sought ahead of her, and with the moon so very far away, the girl was suddenly brought to her knees by a crushing loneliness.

"Why do you stop now?" a voice asked her, though it was so soft she had to wonder whether she really heard it at all.

"Because I do not know what I am doing, or what I hope to achieve by doing it. I am in love with the moon, but the moon cannot love me back. I have seen much more of the world now, and I have also seen that I am no more than a speck of dust floating through it. Why should something as great as the moon care for a speck of dust?"

"Why should something so brave as a speck of dust care what the moon thinks of it?" the voice asked. "I have been with you from the beginning, and I have watched you leave the only home you have ever known to cross forest, ocean, and desert without once looking back. Even before that, I saw you survive a night lost in the snow. You may be mortal, and your life may be fleeting compared to that of those who reside in the heavens, but you are here and you are real–as real as the moon or the forest or the ocean or..."

"The wind?" the girl asked.

"Yes," the wind replied.

And so the girl brought herself to her feet, and the wind walked with her as she forced herself to move across the red terrain. She felt it in her hair and at her back with each step she took, and finally one cliff rose up above all the others in the distance, and she knew where she had to go.

The flowers continued to burn in her hand as she scrambled up the rocks, but she never lost her grip or her footing. As she ascended, the sky darkened and darkened and one by one the stars made themselves known by piercing through it. The girl could hear them whispering, but it did not sound unkind. They were merely curious as to why she had come.

When the girl reached the top of the cliff she saw that there, right at the tallest ledge, stood the moon, waiting for her. Now that she was here, however, she had not the slightest idea of what to say.

"I think she has brought these for you," one of the stars said, and the girl blushed as she stumbled forward and presented her gift.

"They are radiant," the moon said, "and you have traveled quite a ways to be here."

The girl found the courage to explain to the moon why she had come and how she had fallen in love with it, but something shifted inside of her as she did. "Do you remember me?" she asked it.

"I do. I am glad that I could help you. May I ask what it is you desire? If it is my love, then you have it, for I love all who look back at me with the wonder that I have when I gaze at them as they walk the earth below me. Were you to join me in the heavens, then perhaps I could know you and love you as I love these stars, but I dare not ask that of you unless you are certain that you are willing to give up all that the earth has to offer. The decision is yours."

The girl stood there at the edge of the cliff where heaven and earth met, the choice solely in her hands. To live in the sky and be loved by the moon would be a miraculous existence, but what would she be leaving behind for it? She realized that the thought made her unbearably sad, and she found that she already missed the wind for its loyalty and encouragement, and the ocean for its kindness and honesty. She even found that she missed the forest for its snide comments and annoyingly bright insights.

"I am afraid I can't join you," the girl told the moon. "The flowers are yours, but I am unable to give up the earth and all those I would have to leave behind here. My feelings for you haven't changed. I, however, have."

"That is probably the wise choice," the moon said, and its voice was as kind as the girl had imagined it would be when she was first lost in the snow.

When the girl said her goodbyes to the moon, the moon told her she was welcome to visit again, though it knew the journey was a long one. Then, as she descended back down the side of the cliff, she felt the wind brush her face as it welcomed her back. It stayed with her as she returned to the ocean, who was thrilled to see her and hear her story of what had happened, and the three of them talked until the girl reached the shore just before the forest. At this place, where forest, ocean, and wind met, and where the girl could see the moon still glowing above as always, she felt at peace.

"Are you certain that your family will even recognize you now that you have acquired so much new wisdom during your trip?" the forest asked the girl in a gently mocking tone as she walked through it on her way home. "You are practically a sage."

"Careful, or I will build a cottage out of your trees," the girl said, and though she was joking, in time the forest did give her some

of its trees to make a house by the ocean, and then a sailboat so
that the wind could help her make the journey to visit the moon
every once in a while.

In Strange, Far Places

Julia K. Patt

Julia K. Patt does not know what
lurks beyond the stars, but she has
some theories. Her science fiction
has appeared /is forthcoming
in such publications as Escape
Pod, Clarkesworld, and Bikes in
Space. She also edits Seven by
Twenty (@7x20), a journal of
twitter literature-or twitterature, if
you prefer.

On nights likes this, I imagined ours as the only light on REQ.15-337, our distant glimmer just visible to the passing ships return-ing from the far reaches of the galaxy, making their long retreat from our great expansion. The failed colonists could not hear the tinkle of our toasting glasses or the bright bursts of our laugh-ter, but maybe they saw our light, maybe they recognized and cheered the last pulses of life before we abandoned this system for good, as we had abandoned so many others.

There are twenty-nine ships left now, Emeline, my mother wrote me not long before that party. To appease her I knew one day I would board one of those twenty-nine ships docking at 15-337 and return home. I was lucky that someone cared enough to make sure I had passage, I knew. We had all heard the stories of the abandoned REQs in more distant systems, their last few inhabitants cut off from humanity, left to live out their lives in the void until the synthetic atmos failed or the oxygenating phy-tos died or the food ran out.

Most of us left on 15-337 were like that—once too poor to con-tinue the human diaspora into the stars, now too poor to make the long, sad journey home. My flat was filled with the best of these remainders almost every night, a dozen of us reclining on rugs and cushions I'd pilfered from the abandoned quarters around mine, the room warmly lit by my bioluminescent lan-terns. We were a queer, motley, lovely bunch wrapped up in whatever we could scavenge: Zealia curled beside me in a lilac silk kimono; Nix, Slix, and Quix in tight, oil-slick maintenance overalls and tattered top hats; Whipple wearing his bright white plastic suit; Lila and Delora in cut-up transit gear, their long pale legs exposed; Theobald and Humphrey in mismatched officers' uniforms, one too tight, the other much too big; Io and Phoebe in gossamer nightdresses and heavy overcoats; Softly wearing his stern black three-piece as always, unrelieved save for the glittering eyes of its buttons. All of us third-wave expansion brats, born in the deep, pot-bellied transport ships, our parents still believing they were destined to reach the distant stars, colonize new worlds, mine the universe for her secrets. Some of us were mixed Europan, as had been the fashion years before, not half-breeds yet, but enhanced with a few strands of alien DNA, breeding huge dark eyes, gills, or patches of glittering scales into the mix-ostensibly in the hope it would up our chances of survival out in deep space. But I think they just did it because they could. That's why they did everything.

Zealia was one of these, though, and I found her unspeakably beautiful, the scatterings of cerulean scales at her temples, the pale webbing between her fingers, her liquid gaze reflecting my own face back at me. She smiled shyly at me over her glass of phytowine. I meant to take her with me when the time came, although I did not know if she would want to return, a stranger among her own species.

Tonight was one of our quieter parties. It had been that way since the number of ships left to pass through our system dropped below fifty. The last ship to dock had had to use force to keep the REQers from rushing the boarding area. Eight people died. And while there was still food to be had, the gardens and groves at bottom level still plentiful, as the need for personnel dwindled, there were fewer and fewer ways to pay for it. Soon there would be people starving in the streets of the REQ, their lack of credits finishing them off faster than anything in system 15-337 ever could. Even cities in the void died of the same things, it seemed.

Humphrey passed me a pipe; I handed it off to Zealia without taking a hit. I'll board the next ship, I decided. Really, this time, and I would convince my mother to let me take as many of my remainders as would come. Most of the others didn't know I was the daughter of a fleet commander, although I think more of them had guessed than I liked. Maybe it wouldn't matter.

My mother's last message, all out of patience: *Enough slumming. Time to come home.*

Zealia was looking at me, concerned.

"We should tell stories," I said instead of answering her unspoken question. My voice sounded too loud in the room; everyone else had been lost in their own thoughts, too.

Nix—or was it Slix? They were almost identical, androgynous and sharp-featured in the same way—smirked at me. "But we don't have a campfire, Em." Their eyes glittered. "How can we tell ghost stories without the proper...ambience?"

"It doesn't have to be a ghost story," I started to explain, exasperated, but at the same time Softly said, "I know a story."

We all perked up the way we did whenever Softly spoke up. We had named him Softly as a joke, because no one knew his name or nickname or anything about him. "All I know," Io told me when I asked, "is that he speaks softly, walks softly, and looks softly."

"Bet he fucks softly, too," Slix had said, biting their lip and smiling.

He never showed any interest, though, in any of us, with all of our incarnations of self and want and need. Softly was self-contained, troubled yet untroubled, and constant. I was as sure he had an exit strategy for the REQ as I was that he would not leave until the atmo cracked and the void rushed in.

"Our governess used to tell it," he began. We looked around at each other, wonderingly. *Softly had a fucking* governess? I poured my glass full of phytowine, and Zealia snuggled up against my side, her borrowed kimono's synthsilk cool on my skin. We twined our arms around each other's waists.

"In the early days of the expansion, during the first wave, we pushed as far and as fast as we could. We didn't stop to colonize; we mapped every system we found and installed the REQs on dwarf planets and asteroids. Little cities floating in the abyss of space, just like this one."

I saw Nix roll their eyes. "Everyone knows that," they muttered. But Quix and Slix elbowed them in unison and they subsided.

Softly continued: "Every so often, though, the ships would come back through. For supplies or repairs. To drop off the unwanted. Nonessentials. Orphans." Here more than one of his audience grinned. Grimaced. Familiar tales.

Except, perhaps, for me, stowing away on 15-337 when I was seventeen and sick of life careening into the stars and longing for something else, something I could not quite name then. For the misfit REQ children, more like me than the military offspring I grew up with ever were. *Odd, odd Em.*

Softly continued, a sickish smile on his face to match mine. "There was a ship, though, the *Swan*, which never came back. Its last REQ, 20-890, sat on the very edge of unmapped space, waiting. Years passed without word. Of course, it wasn't the first time a ship had failed to return to its REQ. Accidents happen. Space is a dangerous place.

"20-890, in the *Swan*'s absence, prospered. It became like a real city in its own right. Families grew there. They did away with the hierarchies of the fleet, elected their own government. They did away with credits. Everyone worked and everyone had food. At first they thought these would be temporary measures, but the *Swan* never returned and a new ship never came. It seemed, for a long time, like they had been forgotten there, a city on the edge of the galaxy—peaceful, untouched, and happy.

"One day, almost ten years later, they caught the fragmented remains of the *Swan*'s distress signal. It was the only warning they had. They could not decipher the message; they only knew that the *Swan* had signaled for help. And then, they saw it: something so immense that it blotted out the stars beyond the REQ.

"There was no word for what was coming except for *hunger* and that does not begin to capture it. What approached 20-890 was more than hungry; it was all consuming. It seemed, maybe, like nothing, but we all know nothing is a static thing between the stars. It was the void, maybe, if the void had a purpose, a need. It was a *thing* but it was like nothing humans had ever seen before or have seen since. It had consumed the *Swan*; it had even consumed the signal the *Swan* had tried to send, leaving only fragments as a warning. It seemed capable of swallowing stars, it was so impossibly huge and hungry.

"It's said most of the REQers went instantly mad upon seeing it. But before they succumbed, they put a few of the kids in the pods, ejected them toward the nearest system. Only one of them made it. Our governess heard the story from her grandmother, who was one of the kids in the surviving pod. She said she looked back in that moment and saw the REQ be consumed.

Not destroyed, not crushed—just *gone*. Then *it* reached for one pod, then another, overcoming them. It reached for her, she said.

"It wasn't like having a hand reach for you. It was like the nothing was reaching to swallow you. Not like a collapsing star draws everything into it—something that *wanted* to consume you, to draw you in, and unmake you. She looked into it and she swore it looked back, although it was so much more than looking."

Softly paused and regarded the group of us. His voice had grown loud and tremulous as he said this last, and he ran one shaking hand through his wild hair. His eyes were very pale, I noticed, and he wore an insignia I halfway remembered on his lapel.

After he had composed himself, he continued, "When I was older, I looked up 20-890, but the records were redacted. I got flagged for even searching. There have been whispers, though, on the 'net. A few years ago, before they reversed the expansion, though, it happened again. A missing ship, a REQ vanished. Then another. And then the orders came. Retreat. Run."

"We ran out of *resources*," Io said. She didn't sound like herself; Phoebe took her hand. "We spread too far too fast, so they have to regroup."

"Exactly," Softly said. "We spread too far."

"What a boogeyman," Nix laughed. "You said yourself that ships go missing all the time. So do REQs, you know. Asteroids. Solar flares. They're just pebbles floating through space, after all." Confident as they sounded, they took a big gulp of phytowine and shrank between Slix and Quix.

Softly started to respond, but I interrupted, "You wanted a ghost story, Nix. I say Softly delivered. Have you heard the one about the admiral's wife and the Europan?" Without waiting to hear their response, I launched into the sordid tale, complete with limerick.

Later, when nearly everyone had left in whatever configuration kept them warm at night, Softly paused by my door. I regarded him silently, waiting for him to speak. "You should go, the next time you get a chance," he said. "Your mother will be glad to see you."

"What about you?" I asked. I hadn't quite worked out whose kid he was, but I had an idea. There were only so many admirals, after all. "Surely your family—"

"They don't want me. They never did," he said abruptly. He nodded towards Zealia and Io, who were sleeping at either end of my couch like two stray cats. "I'm not different from them. You are, though. You have somewhere to go."

"You could, too," I pointed out. I would write my mother that night, I decided. Ask for as many safe passages as she could offer. Insist. *I won't go without them.*

Softly shook his head. Then, although he never had before, he leaned over and kissed me on the cheek. Gently. Like a brother might.

I haven't seen him since then. Perhaps he does not want to see us, or maybe we have been too busy making arrangements. I am anxious, in the way the others are not, counting down the days until the next ship. I walk the streets of 15-337 at all hours, looking up into the void through the synthetic atmo, so thin, so fragile. The emptiness relieved by the distant stars. Every so often, I think I catch the passage of a shadow through faraway systems. Even from here, it looks big.

It looks *hungry.*

Two Dimensional

Kellee Kranendonk

Living in Atlantic Canada, with her
husband, children and a variety of
animals, Kellee's first publication—
many years ago—was a true story.
Since then she's had several
stories, poems and articles, for both
children and adults, published.
She's also the fiction editor for
Youth Imagination Magazine.

Binya stood on the roof of her building, looking out over the moon-drenched skyline. Even in the dark she could see the smog from the clumped group of unexplainable factories. Although there were groups of these buildings planet-wide, no one seemed to know what they were for. However, what everyone did know was that whoever went in never came out.

Turning away, she pulled a rolled, narrow cylinder out of her pocket and held it between her fingers. She looked at the green, paper-like wrapper for a moment, recalling what Valo, her dealer, had told her. Demetrians, he said, referring to his own race, had been smoking halluphorigens long before humans had come to this planet. He'd insisted the stuff rolled inside the tube was clean, and not the "street shit" most dealers sold. Since Binya had never had a bad experience, and rather liked the places the drug took her, she quickly came to trust Valo.

She placed the cigarette—often called a "'genic" by humans—between her lips and pulled her lighter from her pocket. Slender and sort of an ovular tube, the word *"Bic"* etched into the metal neck, the lighter had come from Binya's grandmother, who still lived on Earth. None of Binya's friends had lighters like this, preferring the reusable ones they could get here on N'Kia.

As she inhaled, the effects were almost immediate. The full moon spun slowly in the sky, like a lollipop on an unseen stick, turned by the invisible fingers of a child. Its light rippled over the surface. She turned back to the skyline. Behind the factories, which now pumped out purple smog instead of grey, stood tall mountains whose tops glittered in the moonshine. She took another drag and the air before her began to ripple and take shape.

She kept smoking until the form resembled a jumbled rainbow of humanoid energy. If she continued smoking, the form would take on human qualities–long, silvery hair, pale yellow skin, and deep brown eyes. But that hallucination had unnerved her so much the first time she saw it that she now stopped when the rainbow appeared.

Crushing the end of the 'genic against the wall of her building, she tucked the cigarette into her pocket. This high would last her for hours.

Leaving the roof, she walked along the street towards the beach. The road rippled with colour beneath her feet as it always did after a smoke. The beach, which normally consisted of soft, brown sand, and blue water, looked so much nicer when she was high. Its water gleamed azure, the sand glittered silver and gold, and the cliffs were striped with rainbow-coloured rocks.

Stepping onto the sand this night, she saw someone kneeling by the water. As the being rose, and turned towards her, she noticed that he looked like Valo except he had that long silvery hair and pale skin of her hallucination.

She smiled and, even though she knew he wasn't real, said hello. To her surprise he returned the greeting, then held out his hand to her. Curled in his palm was a tiny creature, like an octopus with a round muzzle, and one arm longer than the rest. This long "arm" was curled around one of the man's fingers as the creature licked his skin. "It's a sea monkey. She's after the salt in my skin."

Binya looked up into the man's brown eyes. He smiled at her, and then she looked at the little monkey again. Such a funny looking creature, yet Binya wanted one of her own, and where there was one, there had to be more. "You got this in the water?"

"Yes, but–" started the man, stopping when Binya headed to the water. "What are you doing?"

"I want one too," she replied.

"No, you can't–" But before he could finish his sentence, Binya was ankle-deep in the water.

Kneeling, she asked, "How do you catch them?" She remembered a river she'd been to once, so full of fish she could reach in and grab a handful. Real or imagined? She couldn't remember now.

"Please come out of the water," begged the man.

Binya shook her head, laughed, then stuck her hand into the water. Maybe she could just catch a sea monkey.

Suddenly, something bit into her flesh. She screamed out in pain and yanked her hand out of the water. Attached to her hand was a creature with a purplish, cylindrical, jelly-like body. Black wing-like fins stuck out on either side of it. Just in front of those were tiny projections like ears, and below the ears was, apparently, its mouth, or whatever it was using to hold on to her. She shook her hand, but it bit down even harder. "Get it off, get it off," she screamed, leaping out of the water.

The man put the sea monkey on his shoulder and reached out to take Binya's hand in his. He pushed at the ugly, purplish thing but it refused to let go. "I told you to stay put. You got bit by a vampire. They won't bite Demetrians but they seem to have a taste for human blood."

Pain pulsed as she looked at her hand, the vampire's body swelling as it ingested her blood. The man's touch felt so real, his voice sounded strong. She turned her gaze up to him. He glimmered in the moonlight, his body fading in and out. "It hurts, get it off," she whimpered, poking at the thing attached to her hand.

"I can't." He grabbed her shoulders. "Binya, calm down. Calm yourself. Binya!"

He knew her name! Of course he does, she thought as she swiped at the tears on her cheeks, he's just a hallucination. She reached out to touch him, somehow needing to know what a delusion would feel like, despite the pain. As she did, everything around her swirled and she was falling, falling. Then arms caught her. . .

***

Binya awoke in her bed. Before opening her eyes, she took a moment to recall last night's 'genic adventure. Sometimes the memories were hazy, but not this time. Sea monkeys and vampires indeed. Chuckling inwardly, she yawned and then rolled over to look at the time on her alarm clock. She hated when she woke up before it went off. But instead of her clock, she saw her sister, Linny, in a chair beside the bed. A bed which she now realized wasn't hers. "Where am I?"

"The hospital." Linny frowned, and leaned close to Binya. "Why do you do that stuff?" she hissed. "It's illegal and—"

Binya groaned. "Don't start that. Why am I in the hospital?"

Linny ignored her question. "One day you're going to get caught. Then what?"

An image of the factory with its smoke pumping out, and the people that went in but never came out popped into her head.

Maybe that's what happened to 'genic smokers. "Maybe I'll just disappear."

"It's not funny."

Before Binya could respond, the door to her room opened and Valo came rushing in. "Hey, I heard you were in here. How ya doin'?"

"Um, okay." How did Valo know she was in here, and why would he come see her? She glanced at Linny, who glared at Valo with suspicious eyes. Did she know who he was?

"Linny, I'm hungry," said Binya, before Valo said anything more. "Can you get me something to eat?"

Linny rose slowly from her chair, still eyeing the two of them. She opened her mouth as though she wanted to say something, but then changed her mind. Pivoting on her heel, she left the room.

Without a beat, the moment Linny was gone, Valo leaned over Binya and whispered, "You need to get out of here."

She looked at him. A strand of blond hair hung out from beneath a striped toque, and his dark brown eyes stared into hers. The image of the Valo look-alike from her hallucinations flashed into her mind. Then it was gone, pulling most of last night's memories with it.

"Why? What's going on?"

"I don't have time to explain. Do you trust me?"

"Well, yeah," she started.

"Look, if I don't get you out of here, they're going to come and take you away and no one will ever see you again. All because of–" He reached under the covers, grabbed her arm and pulled it free of the blanket. "This!"

Despite the lack of pain, there was a thick bandage around her hand. "What's that?" Foggy images formed in her head again, fading images of sea monkeys and Valo with yellow skin.

"I told you, I don't have time to explain. Come on."

"Can I get dressed first?"

"Where are your clothes?"

"I don't know."

Valo looked around the room, found a small metal locker and opened it. He pulled out the clothes she'd been wearing last night and tossed them on the bed. "Hurry."

"Turn around!"

He sighed, but did as he was told while she changed from the blue johnny-shirt into her clothes.

No one paid them much attention as they moved through the hallways, Valo clinging to her good hand. When they got outside, he led her to a bicycle-powered cart. "Get in."

"Where are we going?"

"I can't protect you from them forever, but I can make it harder for them to find you. They've probably already reported you. I want you to know what's going on before they catch up to you."

"That doesn't answer my question."

"Come on, Binya!"

His desperate tone got her moving. As soon as they both were in the cart, the bicyclist began pedalling furiously. Valo remained silent as they moved away from the hospital. He didn't speak until they were well on their way out of the city. He touched her hand. "Do you know what this is?"

"A bandage on my hand," she deadpanned, trying to lighten the mood. When Valo didn't crack a smile, she asked, "What happened to me?"

"Does it hurt?"

"No."

"Then they have you on painkillers. You don't remember what happened?"

"Yes. . . " she started, but then realized the memories were too blurred to recall in detail. "No. Well, vaguely, but sometimes that happens. How did you even know where I was?"

"I was there, Binya. I know I don't look the same, but I was there. Come on, remember!"

As she looked at him, he pulled off his toque. He shook his blond hair as it fell around his shoulders and framed the lightly tanned skin of his face. Then he took her hand, looked into her eyes and said, "They have a taste for human blood."

Pain slammed into her hand. She gasped and looked down. The pain withered away as she recalled something about a vampire. She lifted her hand, then looked at Valo over the top of the bandage. For a moment, she could see bite marks in her skin as if the bandage wasn't there. But when she looked directly at the bandage, it was gone. "I was bitten," she said slowly, testing each word, unsure if she could trust the memory in her brain.

He nodded. "Yes. Come on, put it all together. I know you got fucked up, but you have to try."

"No," she said, pulling her hand away. "That wasn't real." She turned away from him. She couldn't even remember; how did she know it wasn't real? But she remembered smoking the 'genic. That had been real. And she knew that for hours afterwards, nothing she experienced was real.

"It was Binya. It is. It always is. Just look at your hand."

Betrayal skidded into her heart. She turned back to him, looked directly into his eyes. "You promised me clean 'genics! No street shit!" Tears filled her eyes. What had he done to her?

He put his hands on her cheeks and held her face tight, refusing to let her go, even when she struggled. "I never sold you shit," he insisted. "I always gave you clean stuff.

But everything you know, everything you think you know, is a lie." He glanced at their surroundings. "We're almost there. They will find you, eventually. I can't stop them. But I want you to know it's all a lie. Do you remember what the beach looked like last night?"

"Of course." Even if her memories from last night were gone, she knew the beach well enough, on a high or off.

"That was real, Binya. Real. It's what this place is really like. But this," he said, sweeping his arms in an arc, "this is what they want you to see."

She stared at him. The scenery blurred by in her peripheral vision, scenery that, according to Valo wasn't even real. But how could that be the truth? How could hallucinations be real and reality be. . . hallucinations? No, Valo had to be wrong.

They both sat silent until, moments later, the cart stopped. The cyclist climbed off the bike, kicked down the kick-stand, then pulled out a bottle of water and sat down on the sand. Brown sand, not silver and gold.

Valo climbed down from the cart. "Come on." He held out his hand to her. She stared at it for a moment–his long, slender fingers, pinkish nails. Hands that handed clean 'genics to her, that took her money. He'd never lied to her before, had never entered her high before. Had he come to trust her enough to do so last night? Was she the one to betray him? She took his hand and followed as he led her down to the shore.

At the waterline, Valo waded into the water and plunged his hand beneath the waves. A second later, he pulled it out. A tiny creature sat in the palm of his hand, one long arm curled around his finger, licking his skin.

Valo looked at her. "You see? It's real. The bite on your hand is real. Why else would you have a bandage? That's why I tried to tell you to stay out of the water. Vampires don't bite Demetrians. But I knew you'd be attacked."

Binya's head ached. She still didn't see how this could be true. "But how? Why?"

"Walk with me."

She glanced back at the cyclist. He was back on his bike, riding away from them at a much slower pace. She didn't ask where he was going, or how they would get back. Instead, she turned away and fell into step with Valo.

"Many years ago, when your people colonized this planet, my people already lived here. The problem was we lived on another plane of existence, in another dimension. Even though we could see you, you couldn't see us. It wasn't a problem for most of us. We were content to co-exist with those who knew nothing of us. But our leaders grew frightened.

"Ever since creation my people have smoked 'genics. It was a way of life for us. And, it brought us into this dimension. We can live in both dimensions, but in this one only with 'genics. Our leaders were afraid that our peoples would connect in this dimension, and corrupt our world, fracture our society. Suddenly the 'genics were illegal and we weren't allowed to continue that way of life anymore.

"I . . . I don't understand. You can see us even when you're in your own dimension?" Binya hoped she was asking the right question.

"It's hard to explain, but yes. You're like–" he paused and frowned as if deep in thought. "Like corpses. No, like wraiths, spirits."

"Ghosts?" Not until now had Binya wondered how Valo spoke English so fluently. It occurred to her that if the Demetrians could see them, maybe they could hear them as well. She didn't want to ask.

He smiled. "Yes. That's what you N'kians call it."

Binya pressed her fingers to her forehead, trying to understand what he was saying. "So you enter my dimension when you're high?"

"Yes. But I see it differently than you do. What you saw last night, what you see when you're high, that's reality. That's N'kia as it really is. It's what I see, what all Demetrians see. In both dimensions."

She tried to process this information, but there were so many questions. "N'Kia," she said, her voice barely a whisper. "I'm

N'Kian, and my ancestors came from Earth." She shook her head. "Why are you Demetrian?"

"That's not what we call ourselves. It's only the name your ancestors called us. But that's not important right now. If I get caught here in your reality, I'll go to prison for a long time."

She digested more of the information. "So every time you come into my reality, you risk going to prison."

Valo nodded. "That's why I only come at night. Less chance of being caught."

Then it hit Binya. Her knees went weak. "And every time I'm high, every time I'm in your reality, I risk the same." She dropped to the sand and stared out over the water. He'd known that, yet he'd risked both their lives. And for what? The money? Before she could ask, he sat beside her.

"Yes, but I'm not the only one. There are many of us who desire contact between our people. We risk it because we feel it's worth it, because we want to continue our traditional way of life, because we don't care about the ghosts in our space. We don't fear you, Binya, and we don't want you to fear us."

She wanted to scream at him. He hadn't asked for her permission to take that risk. If he'd told her. . . her thoughts trailed off, her anger subsided. Would she have done anything different? She tossed a handful of sand into the water and watched the grains fall–hallucination into hallucination. No, the water and sand were real. Their appearance was the hallucination, created to protect the Demetrians. But created how?

"Why can I see reality when I'm high?"

"I don't know. We didn't even know humans saw it differently at first. Eventually we figured it out."

She thought about the rainbow energy form, tried to put it into words, but none were exactly what she wanted to say. Nothing sounded right in her head. But she knew now what the form was—Valo, or another like him, coming into focus as she entered their reality, the planet's reality. She held her bandaged hand in the air. Proof. Proof of another reality.

"How did you know I would get bitten?"

"I've seen it happen before. The vampires only bite humans. And when they get bitten, the hospital reports them. Then my leaders know they've been in my reality. N'Kians disappear then, Binya. They don't want anyone to know about the dual dimensions. They work as hard as they can to eliminate the 'genics. And those who know the truth."

The truth! As it all came together in her head, she understood. "The smog," she said. "That's what the smog is for."

"What smog? I don't understand."

As she pointed to a factory in the distance. She realized that Valo couldn't see the smog as she saw it. "Those factories you see, they pump out smog. They're all over the planet. That has to be what keeps us in our own dimension, in their version of it. That's why 'genics are illegal here too. They show us the reality. Our leaders are working together to keep us from realizing it."

Valo nodded in agreement. "They control us that way, and their fear controls them."

"But what —"

Suddenly Valo looked past her and grabbed her arm. "They're

coming, Binya. They must come from those factories. They'll be here soon to take you away and no one will ever see you again."

"But I could have gotten bitten even if I hadn't smoked a 'genic."

"No. The vampires only exist in my dimension."

Her mind whirled as panic rose. A crazy image of the purpley, blobby sea creature trying to bite a ghost flashed in her mind. Vampires and Demetrians in one dimension, N'Kians in another. But Valo was here, in her space. " Do you have something?" she cried, shoving her hands into his pockets. "Hide me! Take me to your dimension."

Valo pulled her hands out, empty. "No, Binya! That won't work. If we get caught over there, we'll still be taken away."

Tears filled her eyes. "What's going to happen to me? To us?"

Valo reached behind his neck and pulled off the little sea monkey. Binya had forgotten about her. He turned to toss her gently back into the sea waves. "I don't know," he said without facing her. "I'm sorry, Binya." He turned back to her. "I can't stay in this dimension, not without another 'genic." He began to fade away. But it was different now that she was straight.

She reached out to grab his hand in an attempt to get into his dimension, but her hand slid through him with little resistance. She heard his last words as if they were nothing but leaves in the wind. "I'm sorry. This was my last. I'm giving up 'genics, Binya."

Their vehicles stopped. Someone shouted. Tears streamed down Binya's cheeks. She turned to face her arrestors as they rushed towards her, shackles in their hands. Falling to her knees, she held her own hands out for them to bind.

The Waiting Room

Carrie Vaccaro Nelkin

Carrie Vaccaro Nelkin writes short stories and poetry and is author of the novel SNARE. She is a member of the Horror Writers Association. Visit her on Twitter @cvnelkin, on Facebook (www.facebook.com/cvnelkin), and on her website, www.cvnelkin.com.

Beatrice Miller closed her eyes and leaned back on the cushions propped against the headboard, listening as Rhea shook pills out of various bottles. She could almost tell which pills made which kind of rattle on their way out.

"Here you go," Rhea said gently, and Beatrice opened her eyes again.

She gazed at the shapes and colors in Rhea's palm: the tiny white one, the brown oval, the fat blue circle, the yellow capsule, the coated pink disk, and the gargantuan greenish thing that looked as if it were made for veterinary use in large animals. She placed one at a time on her tongue and swallowed from the glass of water Rhea held out.

"Let's check your pulse." Rhea sat on the edge of the bed and took Beatrice's hand, the skin fine and wrinkled and soft as only that of the very old can be.

Beatrice searched Rhea's face. "You're not sleeping well, are you?"

Rhea continued counting silently before replying. "It's to be expected, right?" She moved the covers aside to reveal Beatrice's thin legs under the flannel nightgown, her fingers feeling along Beatrice's ankles, then her feet. She seemed satisfied, smiled at Beatrice, and picked up the blood pressure cuff. "Let's do this and then I'll get you some breakfast."

A few moments later Beatrice watched Rhea leave the room. Then she reached into her mouth and retrieved the pills. The white one had melted, leaving a bitter taste, and the blue was half dissolved, but the others were pretty much whole. With some effort she stretched her arm down and stuck the pills between the bed frame and the box spring.

Rhea hadn't opened the drapes. It didn't matter. Beatrice knew what was out there. And they both knew what was coming. It was just a matter of when.

***

Around noon Beatrice asked Rhea to pull the drapes open. Rhea was silent a long moment, then said, "Why? It will only depress you."

Beatrice let out a feeble laugh. "What difference will that make? Here, help me turn on my side."

Rhea helped her. "You probably don't need this extra pillow now." She moved it to the other end of the bed.

"Do you think any day will be better for me than the one before?" Beatrice felt a wrench in her hip and added quickly, "This won't work. I need to get onto my back again."

Rhea's strong arms came to her aid. "Okay now?"

"Yes." Beatrice exhaled with relief. "Open the drapes, will you? I heard more shrieking before. It's like a free-for-all. The hawks, the rabbits, the squirrels—they're all raging at each other."

Rhea clutched her cardigan against her wrinkled nurse's whites. "I don't think you can see anything. The fog just keeps getting worse."

"I need to look anyway."

Rhea stifled a sigh and pulled back her curly black hair with a rubber band she'd plucked out of her pocket." All right, but we should turn the light out first."

Beatrice nodded. Rhea reached for the lamp on the nightstand and pulled the drapes apart. Outside, the fog squatted over everything and pushed against the old house's first-floor windows as if to suffocate all life inside. Thick and gray and aggressive, it reflected dully off the hardwood floor. Rhea kept her eyes averted. At length she crawled into the wing chair in the corner and tried to make herself small in its protective arms.

Beatrice stared into the vapor for a long time. She could make out the larger, closer trees, but everything else flattened into the murk.

"I've been thinking," Rhea said in a small voice. "Maybe we should turn off the generator so as not to call attention to ourselves."

"They'll find us anyway. But it might give us an extra day so you can leave." Beatrice put her face in her hands and sought comfort in the darkness. When she removed them she looked at Rhea and her heart broke. In the large chair the young woman who cooked for her, helped her to the bathroom and changed the sheets when she didn't make it in time, gave her sponge baths and pills she'd stopped taking several days ago—this capable young woman looked like an unnerved child. "There isn't much more time. You have to go *now.*"

"I told you: I can't."

Rhea's eyes were big and shiny. She sniffled, and Beatrice

realized her nurse was starting to cry, something she'd never seen Rhea do.

"I'm not leaving you here," Rhea said.

Beatrice tried to make her voice harsh. "Don't be absurd. What would be the good of even trying to move me? Let's not have this conversation again. How much longer am I going to last anyway?"

Rhea heaved a long, ragged breath filled with tears and mucus. "It's not right. I can't leave you alone." She paused. "I wouldn't even know where to go."

"You don't stand a chance in here, you know. You heard all the reports." The last one had been two days ago.

"It's probably too late already." Rhea reached for the TV remote control, pressing buttons as if to satisfy herself that no stone had been left unturned. The set turned on, but the screen remained black and the volume silent.

"You could try the computer again," Beatrice said.

"Wi-fi's still down."

"Try again. You never know what might change."

Rhea's streaked face showed an uncharacteristic irritability. "You don't think I've been trying every chance I get?"

Beatrice turned her gaze back to the window, searching for new shadows in the haze. There were none yet. "Rhea," she said softly. "I've come to love you as if you were my own child. And I would tell my child to leave me to die in peace and to fight for her life. You can do nothing for me, ultimately, but it would be a sin to go down with me."

"That's not how I was taught."

"Nor was I, but that's the way it is now."

***

A few hours later, Beatrice knew she was awake, understood it was no dream, but suddenly the dusky room with its smells of sickness and its view of the unforgiving fog melted into the backyard of her childhood home, and she was a small girl sitting in the spring-green grass by the pond with the skinny white birch on one side and on the other the Japanese black pines that were so lovely before the blight that would kill them years later. A robin hopped near her in the grass, and she felt the sun on her bare legs. Birdsong filled her ears. Beatrice the girl smiled up at the fluffy white clouds. Beatrice the old woman felt herself heaving with sobs.

Rhea was immediately at her side. "Did you have a bad dream?" She took Beatrice's hand.

Beatrice clutched Rhea's fingers and blinked away the colors and sounds of a different existence. "I'm all right," she said at last.

***

By 5 p.m. Rhea had drawn the curtains again and was in the kitchen preparing a light dinner. Beatrice dozed from the painkiller she'd been given an hour ago. Painkillers she would take. Those, she was not going to remove from her mouth and stick onto the box spring. The room was dark and the house silent, and when the telephone in the hallway rang the sound needled into the old woman's sleep and woke her.

For a moment she didn't know what it was. It rang several times before she heard Rhea running from the kitchen.

"Hello?" Rhea was breathless. "Callan! Callan, where are you?"

Beatrice strained to hear.

"It—they weren't working. I don't know. Is your cell—?" Rhea's voice lowered, and Beatrice could make out tones but no words. She looked at the closed drapes and wished they were open.

She listened for a long time to Rhea's distressed whispering, hearing an occasional "I can't. I can't do that." She would fire Rhea tonight, even though she knew it would be pointless. There was some whimpering from the hallway, then a muffled "I love you." A few more minutes of hushed urgencies followed, and finally Beatrice heard footsteps going back into the kitchen.

In the silence a coarse, heavy sleep overtook her again. When Rhea returned with a tray of soup, toast, and applesauce, Beatrice stirred and pulled herself up slightly. Rhea put the tray down on the small hospital-style table that swung over the bed, then she turned on the nearby light. Her eyes were red and swollen.

"I heard the phone ring," Beatrice said as Rhea tucked a paper napkin under her chin. "Is it working now?"

"I don't know. It wasn't very clear."

Beatrice lifted the spoon halfway to her mouth and waited, but Rhea busied herself smoothing out the bed around the old woman. "Will you have dinner with me?" Beatrice asked.

"Of course," Rhea replied without looking at her. "Just let me straighten up and I'll join you."

Beatrice brought the spoon to her mouth. The soup was a thick carrot and ginger puree. It dribbled down her lip a little but she caught it with a second napkin before it went far. "You heard someone, though. On the phone. Who was it?"

Rhea hesitated. She picked up the empty glass of water on the nightstand. "Callan."

"Your boyfriend?"

Rhea nodded. She seemed reluctant to say more but finally murmured, "He's on the coast. He's found a guy with a boat who's sailing to the Caribbean tomorrow." She clutched the glass to her and glanced at Beatrice.

"He wants you to go with him."

Rhea didn't reply.

Beatrice sighed and put the spoon down. "Go, Rhea. I'm firing you. I have no more money for you. Go."

Rhea looked down at the floor. "You know it's not about money."

"Open the drapes, please." Beatrice's voice choked on a cough and the spasms shook her small frame. "Turn off the light and open the drapes. I want you to see what's outside."

"I know what's outside."

"It's just the beginning. And I want you to know that I've been spitting my pills out when you weren't looking."

"What?" Rhea snapped to attention. "Why, and for how long?"

"The drapes. Please. Now."

Rhea made an exasperated sound and reached for the light,

then she yanked at the clear plastic rod that controlled the drapes. Beyond the window a dense, leaden twilight had settled on the earth, sifting a strange radiance into the fog.

"Look carefully," Beatrice said. "Do you see anyone or anything moving out there?"

Rhea sank to her knees and peered over the windowsill. She stared for a long time before replying, "No."

"That's why you need to go now. Find Callan." Beatrice rested her head back on the pillows and pushed the tray table away. "If I have to tell you again tomorrow night, it might be too late."

To the side of the house a terrified scream cut the fog, tightening into a yowl of anguish that ended abruptly. Goosebumps hatched along Beatrice's neck.

Rhea continued gazing out the window before sitting back on her heels and facing Beatrice. She remained huddled under the sill.

"I don't think I can eat anymore," Beatrice said.

***

She was drawn to the window despite the desperate squeals of rabbits having their viscera torn, their terror lingering like a configuration in the mist. Sometimes she wondered if the cries were from the hawks or maybe the herons or Canada geese that passed through the area. Woodchucks, wild turkeys, deer. . . The caterwauling could be from any of them.

"Wait, you look crooked." Rhea adjusted Beatrice's shoulders against the chair back, settling a pillow between Beatrice's hip and the chair arm. Beatrice winced, and Rhea removed the pillow.

"It's fine." Beatrice bit her lip as she said it. Moving the wing chair by the window and getting into it—her idea, of course— had taken a significant effort, and now Rhea looked as if she were swallowing back an *I told you so.* "Thank you. I'm so tired of being in bed."

"I know. In a few minutes I'll bring your medicine." She shot Beatrice a stern look. "And no spitting anything out."

"Do me a favor. Raise the window for me, will you?"

The look of horror on Rhea's face was instant. "What for? It's almost night."

"I want to smell the air."

"Beatrice." Rhea squatted by the chair and placed her hand on the old woman's arm. "I let you sit here by the window against my better judgment. Why on earth—?"

"It's still my world, isn't it?" Beatrice snapped, then looked contrite.

Rhea stared at her. "Is it? You've been telling me it isn't anymore."

Beatrice pressed her fingers against Rhea's. "Humor me. Just a crack. A few minutes. Then you can close it again." She could almost hear Rhea's thoughts rumbling across the pale unlined face. "It can't hurt me, not at this point."

Rhea sighed and slid open the window lock, then pulled the pane up an inch.

"More," Beatrice said.

Rhea nudged the window up another notch. "That's all. What about me? It can hurt me, can't it? I'm coming back in five minutes." She huffed out of the room.

"Not knowing doesn't make it go away," Beatrice called out, her voice so weak it barely left the chair. Tilting her head, she found the tentative current of air from outside. The smell hit hard and fast, high up in the bridge of her nose, a grimy odor of exhaust, spent fuel, ozone, a combination of things it possibly was and probably wasn't. She tasted the oiliness.

The phone rang, its jangle rattling Beatrice's heart into skipping a beat. Rhea's footsteps pounded into the hallway from the kitchen. The phone rang two more times before Rhea picked up the receiver. "Hello? Callan, is that you?"

Beatrice's eyes skittered over the fog. Against the darkness of the room it seemed backlit. There was something else, something new: a thin, whining screech from deep within the mist. Not an animal sound. A kind of high electrified humming.

"Hello!" Rhea was shouting into the phone. "Hello!"

Beatrice breathed—one breath, two breaths, three. She heard Rhea hanging up the phone.

***

It was earlier than usual when Rhea brought in Beatrice's morning tray. Beatrice had been mostly awake for hours, watching the turbid light of dawn struggle into being. The drapes had been left open all night. The house was chilly, and Rhea wore a thin blue sweater under her cardigan.

"Good morning, Beatrice." Rhea placed the tray on the little table but pushed the table aside so she could sit on the edge of the bed. "How are you feeling?"

Beatrice's smile was weak. "Just peachy, thank you."

Rhea kissed Beatrice on the cheek, then pulled back and gazed at the old woman's face. "I brought you some Earl Grey with your breakfast. A hot cup of Earl always makes me feel better. I put lots of honey in it too, the way you like it." She took Beatrice's wrist and clocked her pulse. Then she pressed a stethoscope to Beatrice's chest and back, drew aside the covers to check for swelling in her legs, and reached onto the tray table for Beatrice's pills.

"How come I get these *with* breakfast today?"

Rhea shook the pills into her hand and held them out to Beatrice with a glass of water. "So there's less chance of your being able to spit them out."

"What's this?" Beatrice pointed at a couple of colossal pills she'd never seen before.

"Pain killer. You're out of the other ones. But you need to take two of these at a time because they're not as strong."

Beatrice eyed Rhea, then nodded. "Can you cut them for me?"

"I thought you didn't like the jagged edges."

"I don't. But these are too big."

Rhea took the butter knife from the breakfast tray and carefully broke the pills in half by pressing the knife against a center dividing line. "You never told me why you've been spitting out your medicine."

The knobby bones in Beatrice's fingers showed white as she clutched the sheet. "So that we can both leave sooner."

Rhea's hand hovered over the pills she'd cut. "I don't like that answer."

Beatrice's breath came slowly. She was immensely tired. "You're young, but at my age, and in my health—" She waved toward the window. "I don't want to be here. I don't want to fight."

Rhea's eyes met hers and they held each other's gaze. Rhea gave the pills to Beatrice and closed the old woman's hand around them. Beatrice put each half on her tongue and dutifully swallowed it with water. She took the other pills as well, this time not removing any of them from her mouth. Rhea poured her a cup of tea from the glazed ceramic pot and buttered the toast for her, placing it next to the single poached egg and three stewed prunes.

Beatrice raised the cup to her lips, her hand shaking slightly. She took a sip and furrowed her brow. "You put honey in this?'

Rhea nodded. "Lots. Why? Does it need more?"

Beatrice took another sip. "It tastes harsh."

"Those new pills I gave you." Rhea got up to straighten the bed around Beatrice. "They can temporarily change the taste in your mouth. Drink up, okay? I'll bring you more honey. Be right back."

She bustled out of the room without looking back.

Beatrice picked up the fork and broke into the poached egg, watching the yolk run on the white plate, the color of the sun as she remembered it. The egg tasted bitter like the tea, and slightly gritty. Somewhere in the house Rhea walked around quietly, a floorboard creaking here, a door whispering closed there. When she finally came back, Rhea held the honey jar in one hand and a glass of milk in the other.

"I warmed this up for you." She placed the milk on the tray and spooned honey into the tea, then sat down in the wing chair. Beatrice noticed she had exchanged her soft white loafers for sneakers. "Might get some of that taste out of your mouth."

Beatrice reached for the glass. "When are you going to leave?"

"What?" Rhea looked startled, the dark circles under her eyes suddenly accentuated.

Beatrice sipped the milk. It left a vinegary sting on her tongue and made her voice lower to a whisper. "You can't save me."

Rhea's eyes wandered carefully over Beatrice's face. "You know I love you, right?"

"I know."

Rhea rose from the chair. "Make sure you eat enough, okay? I can get you more tea if you like."

"This is enough, thank you." Beatrice took another sip of milk, then one of tea and a bite of egg. She dabbed the toast in the grainy yolk, chewing slowly.

"Do you want me to close the drapes?" Rhea asked. "I'll turn the light on."

Beatrice shook her head. "I'm fine. Go make yourself something to eat. I just want to be by myself a bit."

Rhea came close, put her hand on Beatrice's shoulder, and

leaned to kiss her on the forehead. Then she left the room, closing the door halfway behind her.

Beatrice stared out at the fog a long time, sipping the bitter tea and warm sour milk, forcing herself to nibble on toast dipped in the gravelly egg. The prunes tasted all right, and she ate all three. At long last she regarded the empty tea cup and poured herself more, drinking it down in big gulps that tasted less heinous than before.

Finish the milk, she told herself. She stopped with the glass in midair when she heard the click of the front door lock. Very quietly the door opened, halting just before the spot with the chronic squeak. Then silence, and the door closing again with another click and the subtle turn of a tumbler as the deadbolt was set from outside.

Beatrice put the glass down and closed her eyes a moment, falling almost immediately into a doze that splintered when she heard her own battered breathing. Her head was heavy, each rise and fall of her chest an effort.

A great ruckus of squawking and wailing erupted just outside the window. It died quickly and left a shrill keening that bore into Beatrice before falling away.

Her eyes rolled to the window and she saw the shadows of the closest trees, indistinct and little more than smudges, shifting in and out of the opaque brew. She squinted at the movement. Last night's attenuated whine was back, higher, more insistent, cutting through the alarmed bluster of geese somewhere in the distance. Her nose wrinkled at the oily stink creeping into the house.

The shadows grew darker, larger, not trees but vague hominid blurs coming closer, looking less and less like omens or apparitions. Beatrice squeezed her eyes shut, then looked again at the steady, logical progression approaching the porch. She swallowed hard against the dread rising in her chest, then reminded herself it would all be over soon.

She forced herself to drink down the rest of the milk and ran her finger around the bottom of the teacup to gather the last granules. She glanced into the gloom of the bedroom, at the dresser, the unused desk, the old framed photographs of family, and put her head back against the pillows.

She closed her eyes. "Godspeed, Rhea."

Ten Thousand Sleeping Beauties

Jocelyn Koehler

Jocelyn Koehler grew up in the wild, dark woods of Wisconsin, but now lives in a tiny house in Philadelphia that is filled with books, tea things, and places to read, sleep and write. She has worked as a librarian, bookseller, editor, archivist, cubicle drone, popcorn popper, and music store clerk. She has a love for fairy tales, folk stories, and weird, pretty prose.

She floated on tides of stars. She dreamed in constellations and whispered secrets to suns. She flowed in and out of time. She could put it on like a shawl, or fling it out far into the void if she chose. It was bliss.

Then there was pain.

There had been pain at first, too, before the stars and the riding of time. Just a little prick, they had told her. One tiny stab brought an invasion of chemicals charging through her veins, and then her blood exploded into starlight. They said she would sleep, but she didn't feel like she ever slept again. Instead, she sailed through space, indifferent to everything. Until the new pain began.

This pain was different from the first. It was slower. Meaner. It spread over her body, cold water on warm muscles. She shivered, annoyed by it. The shawl of soft time did nothing for her any more. Then the pain grew, spread to her nerves, and pestered her brain. She pulled back from contemplating the cosmos. She breathed in deep, sucking stars into her lungs, and screamed.

"You're awake!" The deep voice reverberated in her ears.

She flinched, opening her eyes to see only the faintest starlight in front of her. "Hello?"

Something searing hot touched her neck, and she screamed

again. Or was it hot? She remembered that burning heat, and realized that it was not burning after all. Touching. That's what it was. Someone was touching her skin.

"You're awake now. Don't be scared," the voice said, more quietly. Something cool wrapped around her throat, dulling the shock.

She blinked, but still saw only dim, dull stars. But who could be out here in the dreamless black with her?

"I looked for you for a long time," the voice went on. Did the bruising, invasive hands belong to the voice? "I had to wake you. I had to try. Are you in...how bad is the pain?"

"Don't touch me," she said, and was now disturbed to hear her words filtered through someone else's voice. A nasty, low, raw voice. Who dared speak for her?

The hands pulled away, and she wondered if she'd drift off again, if anything tethered her now.

"I'm sorry," the voice said. "Your nerves are still reorienting. I underestimated the degree of shock."

"Who are you?" she asked.

"Miji. My name is Olumiji. And your name? Do you remember your name?" The eagerness in that question was so strange. Of course she remembered her name!

"Talia." Again, the rough voice answered for her. She recoiled, prepared to demand that it stop taunting her. Then she understood. "What's wrong with my voice?" she croaked out.

Olumiji said, "It's been a long time since you've spoken, Talia. And you screamed when I woke you. You hurt your throat before I could administer the analgesic gel. We just don't know enough about waking sleepers to know what to expect. It may hurt for a while, above and beyond the awakening itself. Can I give you something else for it?"

"You said you were looking for me," she said, not answering his question—she was sure it was a he now—it was so dark wherever they were...

"Yes. I've been looking for you. All the sleepers. I'm so sorry."

Sorry? Sorry for what? Talia wondered. His phrase triggered something back in the hidden places, where she kept the things she did not need to think about while she sailed out with the stars. All the sleepers...

What had they promised her?

Go to sleep, they had said. Dream through the dark days. Yes. Just a little stab, and she would escape, sail beyond the world into a long slumber. They'd keep her safe the whole time, locked away behind layers and layers of protection. And at the end of it all, in better times, she would be woken. You'll live like a princess, they promised. Still young, healthy, and beautiful...and long past the troubles and strife she was going to sleep through. Her father's voice rose up in her memory. Parents want their children to live a better life than they did. You deserve a saner world than this one. We won't see it, but you will.

She blinked again, but the darkness remained. "Why can't I see you?"

Olumiji asked, "You can't see? You're looking at me."

"I hear you," she said, growing irritated, "but I can't see anything." She lay on some sort of bed or cot, with rough and scratchy fabric.

"The cryo may have damaged your eyes," he said.

She heard the sounds of metal and glass as Olumiji moved nearby. Was she in a medical facility? She had imagined the waking to be different—surely to be done with more ceremony, more joy. Unless something had gone wrong...

"Am I blind?" she asked.

"Don't worry. I'll check the system. Your eyesight can very likely be recovered, either through reconstruction or implants. You'll see."

"Was this complication expected? Did this happen to the others you woke?" She had been assured that her health and safety were going to be closely monitored. "Well? What is the protocol?"

A cough, to buy time. Then, "There is no protocol."

"So who applied for the defrost?" The details of the deal were coming back to her. "Who determined it was safe to wake me?"

"No one."

Talia's heart began waking now, the beats banging together, close on the other. "Then who are you? What happened? What has changed?"

"Things fell apart. I'm sorry."

Things fell apart. Talia felt a flash like a comet slicing through her stomach. "What about me," she said. Not asked. Said.

"I'm sorry."

"What will happen to me?" Surely someone somewhere wanted her. "Where did everyone go? What did the others get when they woke up?"

"I'm sorry," he repeated.

Her breathing was too fast. Did she have to learn that again? How long had it been since she breathed on her own?

"Stop saying sorry!" she hissed. "Where are the others? We'll get together. We'll fight this. It's a breach of contract. Intolerable. There were others in the Spindle!"

Ah, yes, things were coming back now. The Spindle. That was what the facility was called, for the way it was built, and the way it rotated slowly around as it orbited Earth. "There were thousands of us."

"Yes. There were." Olumiji sounded sad. "Ten thousand sleeping beauties."

"Well, what happened to them?"

"Many were lost when the Spindle broke. Not all even survived the initial process. Some survived the cryo but not the thaw. And others were..." He trailed off. "You should rest. I can tell you later, when you wake up again."

"Tell me now. Everything. I've been sleeping. I'm not tired."

He began slowly, unwilling. "The Spindle was in high orbit, and one day...it just broke apart. A meteor, maybe. We're not sure. A lot of sleepers drifted, knocked clear of the gravity well. Others were disposed of, for various reasons. Some were sold as artifacts during the Reconstruction—I'll explain what that is later. One was even installed in a temple, and worshipped. But most of the sleepers just died. The cryo failed early in many units. Not the best craftsmanship. The whole endeavor was quixotic."

Quixotic! Fingers so long frozen now curled up. She would hit him if she could see him. Maybe it was quixotic, but it was the only option to avoid the darkness to come. "How many are left?" she asked.

"I've found dozens of cryo units. But only six sleepers survived."

"Six women survived? Out of all the sleepers?"

"Four women and two men," Olumiji clarified. "The offer was not confined to any particular sex, despite the stories."

"And what do they have to say?"

Olumiji said, "Nothing. I told you six survived. In fact, that only means their vital signs persisted for a while after the thaw."

"They're still sleeping?"

"You are extraordinarily lucky, Talia. I never thought I'd find a sleeper who would actually wake and be...well. The cryo process was never intended to last this long."

A slow, starless cold crept up her spine. "How long has it been since I went to sleep?"

His voice came out low and gentle. "About 450 years."

That was wrong. Talia explained that he was wrong. She explained over and over, louder and louder, explaining quite reasonably despite the pressure against her arms, her chest, despite the shredding of her already tender voice. He continued to be wrong wrong wrong until the pressure grew unbearable and he said she must not fight him. Just like the first time, something stabbed into her that made the sounds all run together and go far away. She heard Olumiji calling, "It's okay. It's only to keep you from hurting yourself. It's okay."

It was not okay. She hated him. Then she slept.

They must have done something to her. When Talia woke up again, lethargic and cranky and aching in body, it took her a few minutes to understand what changed.

Hazy shapes now floated in front of her. Light and shadow. She blinked and almost saw a window, though she could not see beyond it.

"Olumiji," she said. A name she did not like, but it was the only name she knew. Her throat felt a bit raw, but far better than before. "Olumiji! Where are you?"

"Talia?" Olumiji's voice came into range. "Are you well?"

She blinked rapidly, struggling to see a shape to match the voice. "Miji! I can see..."

A vague outline of a person came into her view. Slowly, it resolved into a real person, not just a shadow. Hair prone to curling was cut close to his scalp, and his skin was dark brown. The eyes that now looked back at her were even darker, nearly the color of space.

"You can see now," he said, showing white teeth.

She smiled back, feeling infinitely better that she was not just speaking into a void. She could see perfectly. "Did they fix my eyes? How?"

"I did. A simple procedure. The cryo induced cauling—your eyes filmed over in an effort to prevent frost damage. I used a laser to remove the cauls." He paused. "I hope I did it right. Were your irises pink before?"

"Pink!" Talia gaped.

"Joke. Your eyes are green." The sound of his laugh rolled around her horror and teased her until she didn't even know what words to hurl at him.

When she opened her mouth, she was shocked to hear her own laugh burst out of her. It felt good. She hadn't laughed in centuries. Then a wave of fatigue shook her body. But she asked Olumiji to keep the needles away from her.

He said he would; she didn't need them anymore. Miji told her he thought she would recover fully, and the doctors he spoke to over the ansible were optimistic.

She finally understood that he was not a doctor at all. "What are you, then?"

"A scholar. I am known for being the man who believed in the story of the sleeping beauties. That's why I got this ship."

"Ship!" Talia said. "Where are we?"

"Twelve days out from Ceres. That's about where I picked up your unit's signal."

"I thought we were on Earth!"

"Ah...no. As I said, the Spindle broke between two and four decades after you went to sleep. A lot of the units drifted."

"No one came after us?" she asked, outraged.

"Considering what was going on Earth at that point? Wars? Famine? No. The loss of a few thousand sleepers was negligible. And inefficient to rescue."

"Our safety was guaranteed."

Olumiji made a sound that wasn't quite rude, but made her skin grow hot.

She said, "That was the whole point. To stay safe until we woke."

"I'm sorry it didn't work out for you."

Talia didn't have the strength to face his sarcasm. "So we're in your ship now."

"This is the Errant. It's not my ship, but I'm allowed to use it to search for any sleepers."

"Why you?"

"I've always been interested in the story. Thousands of souls so unwilling to live in the coming dark ages that they chose to sleep through them. Of course it didn't end well. It was like one of those episodes in school that they told a ghost story. Most people didn't believe it really happened. Just propaganda to vilify the decadence of the previous age. But I kept reading, whatever I could find. I studied the whole incident.

"I found stories from different places that seemed to match. I learned that the Spindle was real, and then found out about the break. There were some floating objects in high orbit that turned out to be cryo units, but they'd never been properly identified. However, I knew what to look for. I found empty shells, blown apart by impacts or just busted from a bad frost. I had to look further out if I was going to find any sleeper to reawaken.

"I used any spare ship I could. I went on one week, one month trips, looking for pings that matched the tracers from the Spindle. Then I found one intact unit. I woke a sleeper. Overnight, everyone went from calling me insane to calling me an insane hero. It was unreal."

"What happened to her?" Talia asked.

Olumiji shook his head. "She died very soon after, due to

complications from the thaw. I was afraid to wake the next one I found. I asked for guidance, but who could say? Is it better to dream forever, or be woken and risk death?"

She didn't answer, not knowing herself.

He visited every day while Talia slowly gained strength. He was the only visitor, because he was the only one on the ship until he found her. Talia didn't mind. She thought that if she had a hundred visitors, Miji, with his quiet voice and sudden smiles, might still be her favorite.

He fed her the same rations he ate himself. Talia, though ravenous, wrinkled her nose at the odor the first time. "Why does this smell like a wet sponge?"

Olumiji smiled. "It's mycological. Fungus based. Quick to grow, low light requirements."

"We eat fungus because we're shipboard?"

"We eat fungus because it's food," he said. "With rice, of course. What did you expect?"

"In space, I don't know. If I were home..." She remembered a taste on her tongue with abrupt clarity. "The last thing I ate before I went to sleep was wild salmon, with potatoes and lemon and greens, and chocolate cake for dessert..." She stopped, because Miji's hoot of laughter filled the whole ship.

"Salmon. Wild salmon. Oh, that's..." He struggled to speak through his mirth. "You ate salmon!"

"Why is that funny?"

"You might as well have eaten gold. You might have dined on a tiger. The big fish...they're nearly gone, Talia."

She smiled at him, but wondered if she should have woken at all. Earth without real food... She ate the dull meals she was offered, and began to dread her return to the world.

She grew stronger. She sat up. She learned to walk again, and with Miji's hands to guide her, it was easy. Miji showed her the ship, a tour that took all of twenty minutes. It was like living in the veins of a great beast. The passages were dim. The central one that ran from the bridge to the engine room was circular and fairly wide, but the few passages off it were narrow knife-wounds that accommodated only one body at a time. The rooms were brighter, since functionality demanded it. The infirmary was the largest room after the bridge, and the best lit, even sporting a therapeutic sunlamp.

Four sleeping coves nestled along the top ridge of the main corridor, and a tiny mess hall at the end held a nook with a table, where all normal leisure activity took place. Talia could not imagine four people stuck on this ship.

All the rest of the space was given to storage, food, and air and water processing. And the part of the ship that was not space was packed with guts and nerves of wire, the chips, the dedicated systems that made it possible to live in the great nothingness surrounding them.

On the bridge, they looked at the screen showing the deep dark the ship swam through. She asked how long it would take to get back to Earth. With an apologetic gesture, he said eight months at minimum. Miji explained that to save fuel, the Errant was traveling in a long arc that mimicked the paths of the planets. Only if he found a signal that might be a sleeper did he spend extra fuel to chase after it. The ship didn't have the capacity to travel quickly...that was reserved for high-priority missions.

For the same reason, communications—while fairly regular—were intermittent. The ansible was powerful, but cost energy to operate. The crisis of Talia's waking had taken up much more of the ansible's time than had been expected.

She spent a few days slowly acquainting herself with her tiny new world. One door was locked. Talia tried to open it several times, while Miji was on the bridge. It defied all her attempts.

"What is behind the locked door?" she finally asked.

Olumiji didn't take his eyes from the main screen. "The cargo hold."

"Why is it locked? Are you afraid I'm going to steal something and run?"

"The other sleepers are there."

Talia pulled back. "There are more?"

"Not like you," he said quickly. "They're iced."

"I want to see them."

With a sound of defeat, Olumiji took her. He unlocked the door, and though he put a cautionary hand over hers, Talia dashed inside.

Talia stood in the frigid cargo bay, staring at a half dozen cryo shells standing upright on the floor. Each one held a sleeper, with a face barely visible behind a circular pane of absurdly thick glass. It was like looking at a body below ice, or a wavering reflection of one about to be pulled out to sea.

"Why haven't you woken these ones?"

"I tried," he said, his voice hot in the freezing hold. "I failed. It was too late for all of them."

"Who are they?" she asked, her voice trembling. "Their names, I mean?"

"I don't know." Olumiji walked to the rightmost unit and touched the shell. "There's a number on the side, but I don't know what the number links to. So much was lost."

"What will you do with them?"

"Take them back to Earth," he said. "My supporters need to justify the expense of these excursions. The sleepers are artifacts. They'll be studied."

"They're not artifacts. They're not objects," said Talia. "Would you have sent me back to be studied?"

"You're different now," he said. "You woke. And I know you a little..."

The last unit on the left had no face behind the glass. It was darker than night, darker than space. "That's mine, isn't it?" she said. "You were saving it in case I died too! You would have sold me with all the others."

"Not sold, Talia..."

"You would! I see it. You're just in this for...salvage. I hate you." Talia fled, ignoring his words following her, and she never went into the cargo bay again.

She would have avoided him completely, but how could she in such a tiny world? They ate the same food, breathed the same air, passed each other a dozen times in a day. Too furious to speak, she instead haunted the ship, waiting until Olumiji left the bridge to slip into it, or shadowing him down the narrow passages so that she wouldn't encounter him eye to eye.

However, Talia had been alone much longer than Olumiji had. She had to speak, to hear her voice outside her head. On the bridge, she found a way to use the daily log to record whatever she wanted to say, and soon a torrent of the past poured out of her and into the ship's memory. She spoke about her childhood, growing up in glass towers. She talked about the world she remembered, the ever-increasing danger and fear she heard about every day. She talked about how she couldn't sleep at night, how her mother and father woke her from nightmares. She talked about the day she first heard about the Spindle, and realized there might be a way to avoid the terror. To skip like a stone over the darkest waters.

She steadfastly ignored Olumiji, but when she began to talk about the sleepers and about the Spindle, his attention became too much to bear. She raised her voice at little. She let him listen. He stopped nearly everything else he was doing to hear her speak. His hunger was obvious, but he never asked a thing.

One day, though, he did speak to her. "Talia, there's a request from Earth. Not from me, I'm just the messenger. Will you hear it?" he asked.

She nodded stiffly.

"They know you're here. They know you're awake and fully functional. The doctors who helped me reported the news, as they had to. But now it's got out, and there are so many people with questions for you. Would you answer some of them?"

"I've recorded hours of logs already," she said. "Have they not listened to all of those back on Earth?"

He looked nervous, embarrassed. "The recordings don't get sent anywhere by default. I didn't send them over the ansible. I've haven't let them be shared yet, because I'm a miser."

"Miser?"

"I found you," he said, his voice fierce. "I woke you. Why should everyone else get to hear your words and write their papers and their stories and their opinions of you before we even get back to Earth?"

"You're hoarding my life?" she asked, though in truth she was rather touched that he thought it worth hoarding at all.

"I am, and not all for selfish reasons. Why should you give away the one thing you have?"

"What does a 450-year-old homeless woman have that your society wants?"

"Memory," said Miji, as if it were obvious.

"Memory?"

"You can tell these stories of your growing up in your tower of glass. Why you became a sleeper, what led you to it. Tell people what it was like in the last days of the old world. You were there!" His eyes were bright. "Think of it. You carry a treasure inside you. Everyone will want to know all about your life."

"Including you," she reminded him. "That's why you searched for us all, isn't it?"

"Yes. But your story is yours. I found you, but you should speak to who you want."

Talia watched him for a long moment, saw his mingled pride and fear.

"I will speak to you," she said, and was gratified by a caught breath, perhaps the same sound a reader makes when a mysterious passage becomes clear.

Though Miji had kept her recordings private, the news of her waking was indeed out. From the ansible came greetings and blessings and questions. The Errant couldn't rush back to Earth, so her future arrival was like some marvelous holiday—on the calendar but not to be rushed.

And in the meantime, they had so many questions. Some were cold, academic queries. Others asked about her dreams. Children asked if she knew what milk rice was. She did not, but she told the children about salmon, and explained that chocolate had been drowned in sugar as an everyday treat, not the bitter medicine Miji told her about. The children's flood of replies nearly shut down communications.

Soon, marriage proposals came to her, from people who'd fallen in love with the idea of a sleeping beauty. She declined them, and they accused her of having a frozen heart. Others offered to honor her with their patronage. She didn't answer any of them, for she had no interest in those who would wait for her to arrive like a cargo ordered from a far-off land.

Some offers shocked Talia with their boldness, and others Miji refused to even let her see, his dark complexion not doing a thing to hide his feelings. She teased him at first, but she soon grew shy when the subject came up. She realized her heart was not frozen at all.

One day, Talia had a proposal of her own. After she convinced

Miji that it was not merely the fact that she'd been alone for 450 years, or that he was the only human she knew since her awakening, he accepted her proposal with a joy and a greed that made her laugh. After that, the ship never seemed too small.

Neither Talia nor Olumiji ever mentioned the silent sleepers in the bay. Instead, they talked to each other about each other, conversations that would have bored the rest of the world to tears. But they cared very little about the rest of the world in those first few precious weeks.

Eventually, he told her more, especially the slow climb up from the dark days and the new civilization that emerged. "You'll see, Talia," he said of his Earth. "It may not look like the world you left, but it is better. Brighter."

Talia looked out at the stars. "But I don't know anyone there. I have no place."

He said there was no way to hurry back, and they could live on the ship for years, if needed. So they searched for more sleepers set loose from the destruction of the Spindle.

Talia had such hopes that one would awaken and be another who could speak like her. But most were long past helping. A few seemed like they might wake and recover. One young man with hiragana characters inked up and down his arms even took a single frost-ridden breath. But inevitably, vital signs grew unstable, and the sleeper slid into death. Talia was the only one of her kind, Miji said.

Talia didn't care about returning to Earth, and Miji said he was selfishly pleased to stay in the black with her.

Months slipped by, and she was happy. Even when her eyes began to cloud at the edges, she was happy. Even when her bones ached a little, all the time, she was happy. She began to shake, and then she could no longer walk without putting her hands on the walls, but she was happy.

It became clear that she had not escaped the dangers of the too-late awakening. Miji put her in the infirmary's scanner and sent the data to be read by far away doctors. Even when she and Miji read the medical report that held no good news or hope, she was happy. She loved the tiny world she lived in and the one she lived with. So long as he was there to wake up with her and help her walk the narrow passages of the ship, and to talk with her while they stared out at the ancient light of stars just now reaching their eyes, she was happy.

Miji was happy too, for her. He said he was saving his rage and sorrow for the time after she left him alone again.

When they both knew the end was close, when she could only lie in the bed and hold his hand, he asked what she wanted.

She told him. "Let me go. Don't make me into a specimen of the old days, like the other sleepers in the bay. Let me go."

He said he would, and in return, she told him the future.

Talia told him that when she at last closed her dim and fragile eyes, Olumiji would take her body in his arms. It would be easy, because she weighed so little. Her cold-ravaged bones were now as hollow as a bird's. He would put her back into the capsule that he'd found her in, the one that sat empty in the bay ever since. No need for the cryo to work now...he would lay her body out and kiss her goodbye.

Talia told Olumiji that the capsule would sit in state in the airlock for two days. Olumiji would need that long to give the command

and let space in, and the sleeping Talia would need that long to set his soul properly in her dreams.

But at last he would give the command, and with no sound, the sleeping beauty would drift out on a tide of stars, to dream in constellations and to whisper secrets to suns.

Olumiji would then turn the Errant sunward, for the long, silent running back to Earth. Others might decide to search for the sleeping beauties of legend, but he wouldn't look for any more. He would live on the bright Earth, and make it brighter. And Talia would have no other dreams.

All happened as she said, for he had awoken her, and she had learned to see.

Far, Far From Land

Jude-Marie Green

Jude-Marie Green is a writer of genre (science fiction & fantasy, plus the occasional horror) fiction. She lives in Southern California amid palm trees, orange trees, avocado trees, roses, and birds. Lots of birds.

So the spaceship slewed sideways from uncorrected gravitational pull and shuddered from an unexpected gust of solar wind that stirred the heliosphere. Windows of dimensional matrix display lit up and the xyz grid showed the wave of force. Navigator Rex at the helm commanded the ship's response but couldn't correct in time. A full pot of juicy fractals bounced out of the unsecured magnetic grapple and slithered across the side of the ship and back into the void, free once more.

"Damn-me," Capn Jacq said. "We just lost a fortune in mandel-brots. Rex, you asleep over there?"

Navigator Rex didn't look up from the data streaming onto his window. Deckhands struggled to reel in the line. The pot dangled in space, empty as a suit of clothes.

"Watch the hydraulics!" Capn Jacq roared. The winch squealed as it drew in the line, dragging the pot behind it. Too fast and the pot would launch into the ship's hold rather than be neatly caught up again.

"You've done this before!" she bellowed into the comm. Broadcast volume pegged in the red zone. "Reel it in, hook it up, toss it out. Fifty times a day! Seven days a week! Six weeks a season! A little rough sea is part of the fun. Get your thumbs outta your mouths and pay attention!"

Deck crew—four of them clumsy in counter—pressure suits, two safely behind poly netting controlling the hold 'droids—stowed the line and brought in the empty pot. The greenhorn, newest kid on the ship who thought she could handle space and EVA and grinding hard work on the fishing vessel, clambered into the pot and reset the come—hithers, electronic pied-pipers that called to the mandelbrots. The greenhorn—Capn Jacq checked the shift list: this one was Mackenzie Lutz, female, out of Luna Colony (limited)—worked fast and was getting the hang of it all. Capn Jacq thumbed the greenhorn's record and placed a pip by her name.

"All right already, launch that puppy!" Capn Jacq pushed the clarion button and the hold light flashed green. Green for go, green for release, green for all the money she would make from a hold stuffed with fractals.

Capn Jacq studied the fishing calendar she already knew by heart. Mandelbrots, the current crop, were big and brought in plenty of cash for their size; in two months the julias would be in season, a lot smaller but much more lucrative, also much harder to catch; and next year sometime the quota for quaternians, wheel shaped and hardest to catch, would be set and her ship, Spaceship F/V *Northern Star*, would make another fortune, trawling the asteroids for the luxury foods industry.

She'd lived all her life in space and loved the acidic savor of fractals. Who would have thought that those wild organic crystals were food? Who was the brave soul to first cook one up, microwaved, steamed, drizzled with oleo? Then again, back on Earth, who was the first to eat a snail?

Her well-trained crew worked to bring in another pot, this one locked closed and half-full of mandelbrots. The ship stayed quiescent while they grabbed the pot. One of the droid operators attached the suction hose and the fractals drained away into the ship's refrigerator. Warmed up from the near-zero temperature of open space, the creatures plumped up and quieted down. On deck, the greenhorn reset the come-hithers and the hands tossed the pot back into space.

Capn Jacq tagged the location on her map. Pot 19 of 60 on this string, smack dab in the middle of the asteroid belt biomass migration from MA52 to MA06. Six other spaceship fishing vessels had rights to fish these fractals, plenty of ground to cover in those thousands of square miles of space, plenty of fish in the sea. So to speak.

Another jolt upended the ship. Navigator Rex's holo fluttered.

Capn Jacq plugged in overrides and allowed emergency subsystems to correct the ship's skew and lay.

"Rex, what the hell was that?"

The navigator licked his lips. "Unexpected gravitational thrust from behind us, captain," he said. "Looks like an unremarked asteroid is hoving fast up from behind MA52. It will overtake us in eight."

"Well let's see if we can avoid it," she snarled.

"Yes, ma'am," Rex said. "Captain? The deck. Looks like someone's overboard."

She'd missed the klaxon in the flurry of other demands on her displays. Three deckhands held tight to harnesses attached to one of the droids. The second droid launched itself after the floating deckhand.

"Who is that?" She scanned the telem. "Damn, it's the greenhorn. Wouldn't ya know. Did we lose the pot too? Maybe she can reach the pot."

She studied the windows. "Can't see anything on these things!" She flicked on her comm to the droid pilot.

"Marco, there's an asteroid about to buzz you. Keep a tight grip."

"I'm out on a limb here, Capn Jacq, let's see if I can stretch." He hummed something. She knew the racy lyrics but didn't want to think about *that* right now.

"Fer gods' sakes, Marco, *status!*"

"Oh that's one big piece of rock," Marco said conversationally.

Capn Jacq thumbed off the line to Marco.

"Rex?"

"Reasonable distance," he said. "We're sliding away from it."

Capn Jacq opened the line to Marco.

"Marco? Enjoy the view but don't sweat it. It's passing by. Get the greenhorn. And the pot."

"Yeah, Cap, I'm about five meters away from the ... got her! No problems, easy-peasy-mac-n-cheesy."

"Think you can snag the pot?"

"Sure, I've got one waldo free. The jet spray is a little low; we'll have to refill when I get back." He hummed a tune while he maneuvered. "Got it. Returning to the ship."

"Good work, Marco. Okay, did you guys copy that? He's coming in. Stand by to assist."

She watched the droid settle onto the deck. The other hands

abandoned the safety droid. Two went to secure the pot, the third helped the greenhorn off the deck.

Cap'n Jacq said, "Okay, guys, Rex says it'll be about an hour to realign into our flight path. Take a break, stretch your legs. Don't smoke 'em even if you've got 'em."

The hands crammed into the airlock while the droid operators docked the machines against the deck hull. In just a few minutes, the deck was deserted and neat, open to black jeweled skies of asteroid belt space.

Capn Jacq spun her seat around to face Rex. "Now us, we don't get a break. We have to wrestle this ship back onto path."

Rex grinned. "Sure, Captain. No problem." He played with his window, touching the lines he wanted. "Captain, you need to look at this." He expanded the virtual view of the fishing ground. "That rogue asteroid left a mess behind it."

Like cream stirred into a cup of coffee on a full-gravity kitchen table, the rogue asteroid had stirred the biomass from its normal dense herd. Now two main herds swirled in space, each roiling opposite the other. The fractals were swimming away from the path of the asteroid and away from her string of pots.

Capn Jacq knew a lot of cuss words. Over the next few minutes she used them all and made up a few. When she wound down she took a deep breath.

"All right, Rex, we've gotta pick 'em up... empty, I guess... and put 'em back down again. You got it covered?"

"Sure," he said. "I can plot a path. But the swirl of the biomass hasn't resolved yet. They may change up again."

"Are they coming back to this line?"

"I don't think so. Looks like the rogue swept them away."

"Then we need to set a new line."

"Captain, that would bring us into Captain Phil's quadrant."

She spun her chair a few times, 360s, faster each rotation. "Fine with me. Where's Phil now?"

"I'll ping him," Rex said. His window glowed with bright blue spots surrounding the *Northern Star*'s position. Some of them had tags: F/V *Cordelia Marie*, F/V *Magician*, F/V *Water's Edge*. Two blue spots were untagged but away from the biomass.

"Where's the *Beowulf*?" Capn Jacq said. "I know he's out there. He's supposed to be right beneath us."

"Hailing," Rex said. The one word held all the tension in the world.

"Yeah, SOP," Capn Jacq said. "Put it on the monitor. And speaker. I wanna hear Phil's voice."

"*Northern Star* calling *Beowulf*, come in," Rex said. His finger marked the *Northern Star*'s avatar on the window and trailed to the cluster of tiny brilliant lights underneath it. The rogue asteroid had traveled on that trajectory.

"Come back, *Beowulf*," Rex said.

***

The miniscule kitchen and dining area held all six deck hands plus the cook. They sat close enough to feel each other's bodies from knee to shoulder on both sides. Mackenzie lifted her coffee from table to mouth, jostling the man on her left, and drank. No delicate sips. She wouldn't be delicate with these rough spacers.

Still, the coffee tasted fine, not the sludge she'd expected on board a spaceship fishing vessel.

"I owe you a round of drinks," she said. She ran her right hand across her freshly-shaved scalp. The stubble felt like velvet.

"Yes, soon as we make port," one of them said. Marco? He'd rescued her. Talked a lot. She had him pegged as the crew ringleader. "It's tradition. The greenhorn goes open space at least once a season." He glared at the others. "Not that the crew's supposed to let the pot go. I'd have been after it even if you hadn't gone flying." He smiled at her.

She liked the smile.

"All right, when we get back to Luna Colony, I know a place," she said. "Bar in front, bunks in back."

Skinny Pete, a long-time deck hand, laughed. "None of that! Didn't they tell you? No shipboard romances!"

"Not unless you're Captain Jacq!" More snorts of laughter.

"Stow it, kiddies," Marco said. "She took care of that problem. That's our Captain Jacq, a problem solver if ever there was one." He shook his head.

"Captain Jacq fell in love?" Mackenzie poked at the communal plate of eggs the cook had set in front of them.

"Don't you agree she's a lovely woman?" Marco said.

The crew agreeably rumbled in the affirmative.

"Phil thought so too. Good ol' Phil," and Marco shook his head again. "I've never seen a guy get it so bad as when he first set eyes on Captain Jacq. Of course, she wasn't a captain then, but neither was he."

"What happened?" Mackenzie asked, because she knew she was supposed to ask. He'd have told her even if she'd stayed mute but he wouldn't have been as pleased. She wanted him to stay happy.

"What do you think happened? They snuck away at all hours, finding all the weird, uncomfortable, *secluded* spaces of the ship. Later on, Captain Phil mapped them all out for the ship's metrics. Captain Jacq swears they kept a couple secret, just in case."

He winked at the greenhorn. She blushed and swallowed more coffee.

"After a while, Captain Luke... that's Captain Jacq's dad, God rest his soul."

The crew all repeated, "God rest his soul," and Mackenzie ducked her head and said the words too.

"Captain Luke got wind of the affair and boy was he furious. He swore up one side and down the other that he'd send Phil so far away that the sun would nova before his daughter saw the likes of him again.

"Captain Jacq and Phil had to own up to Captain Luke that they'd gotten married at the last port and if Phil was sent away, she'd follow him. 'To the ends of the galaxy,' she said, and if you'll notice that's our ship's motto." Marco leered at her a bit then winced. "Hey! Who kicked my leg?"

"Just get on with the story," someone said. "Girl's gotta know."

"Captain Luke swallowed his pride and retired, giving his ship over to his daughter and her husband. Captain Jacq and Captain Phil!" They all gulped coffee in a toast. "But a ship can't do with two captains, even two in love as completely and utterly as Captain Jacq and Captain Phil. After a while the two got to squabbling and countermanding each other's orders and things were a fine mess." Marco frowned. "I think they woulda split up, despite being god-damned in love, if Captain Luke hadn't mortgaged his retirement pension and bought a fishing vessel for Captain Phil."

"To Captain Phil!"

"To the *Beowulf*!"

"And it's good for us too," Marco continued. He winked at her. "Crew gets sick of each other, ya know? So whenever someone is done here, they can get a bunk on the *Beowulf*, as long as someone there wants to switch. We're brothers!"

"Ahem," Mackenzie said, pretending to clear her throat.

"No, really. Brothers. Even the ladies amongst us. When you aren't green any more, you'll do the blood brother thing with us.

"Of course, *Northern Star* is a better ship, and Captain Jacq pulls in bigger catches and makes more money for us all. But *Beowulf* is a good change."

"Oh now, *Beowulf* is better during the julia season, and those are pricier fractals, better paychecks," a woman who'd recently worked on the other ship said.

The warning bell rang.

"Time for shift," Marco said. He grimaced when he looked at his watch. "We're early."

The cook said, "All right, all you outta my kitchen!" She shot an evil grin at Marco and Mackenzie. *No time to fool around now,* the grin said.

"Attention crew. Attention." Rex's voice poured through the speakers. "A ship was hit by that last asteroid and we are changing course to intercept. Ship involved is *Beowulf.* Repeat, *Beowulf.* No hails to the ship's frequencies have been answered. No SOS has been received from the area."

Capn Jacq's voice took over. "All right. To the deck. Secure it for rescue operations. Arrival to area of debris... "—her voice shook— "last known location of *Beowulf* in two hours. Hustle, people."

***

Capn Jacq hugged herself when the ship arrived at the last known coordinates of the *Beowulf.* Mandelbrots overflowed the sky, rich fishing, the pointy shapes full and round. The backwash of the asteroid would clear the fractals to another path soon. She'd never be able to catch them. She didn't care. She only wanted to see the debris that comprised the remains of the ship.

Not the debris, she thought. *Lifeboats. There will be lifeboats. There are always lifeboats. Phil will be in one.*

Rex told the display to mask out the fractals. He looked for larger biomasses amid the ship debris signatures. Bright red speckles showed up in a clump in the display.

The mass analyzer said that the apparent spots of highlighted biological material accounted for eight people's worth of mass. At least two bodies, maybe three, shy of the full crew.

Eight people were in space. Free-floating.

Rex said, "Captain, I found a lifeboat. Locked in route to intercept. Arrival five minutes."

"How many?" she said.

"Two," he said. "Telem shows that they're alive. Can't raise them on the hail, though. Their radio must be out."

"Names?" *Is it Phil?* Her finger hovered over his name on the crew list.

"Will let you know. Crew, stand by to open hold door."

The deck hands did the work quietly, no cross-chatter on the comm.

Capn Jacq's fingers pounded over the comm desk, sending messages, receiving messages, logging officialese for the inevitable inquest. She corrected a typo.

It has to be Phil.

Her crew opened the doors to the deck and spotted the lifeboat. That was a standard-issue vehicle, bright orange, cigar-shaped, big enough for ten people for ten minutes, the joke went.

The crew secured the lifeboat with magnets and toggle lines. The greenhorn, Mackenzie, pounded on the lifeboat hull in Morse code, warning the survivors to don their vacuum suits. She repeated the message. After a pause, she started the message again but was interrupted with banging from inside the lifeboat. They'd heard. They'd understood.

The survivors twisted the hatch open and climbed out. Two deck crew helped them out, awkwardly dancing over hatchways and tank openings.

Capn Jacq rumbled, "Who do we have here? Sing out, spacers!"

"Duchovny."

"Anderson."

Of course it's not Phil, she thought. *He'd never stay safe while others floated.*

"Welcome aboard!"

For just a moment the spacers, hers and the *Beowulf*'s, stood motionless. Then with shouts of glee they fell into a group hug.

After a suitable pause Capn Jacq said, "That's enough of that. You two, into the ship. Med check. The rest of you, back to work. Let's get the rest of the crew."

Instantly sobered, the crew stared into space open above their heads. Up there were eight spacefaring fishermen. Friends. Brothers. And Captain Phil.

"Aye, aye, ma'am," Marco replied.

Someone, probably Marco again, had the bright idea of using the pots for recovery. Swarms of fractals and the floating cloud of ship debris and bits of shattered asteroid hindered crew struggling to grasp frozen and slick suits, some with hasty red emergency patching. As the crew scooped them up, they read out the identification numbers. Rex listed the numbers, checking off the recovered survivors.

"I'm going down there," Capn Jacq said.

Rex frowned. "You belong here. The command chair can't be empty during an emergency."

"My ship, my rules," she said. "Keep it together, Rex."

She stood in the gangway, draping mylar blankets around quickly-unsuited crew and sending them to the mess.

"Coffee," she said. "All the coffee you can swill. You know the way." She patted backs and shook hands and even hugged a couple of the long-timers. But her eyes were distant and she stared over their shoulders, looking for someone who wasn't there.

Rex announced, "All right, that's it. We've recovered everyone. No more human-sized biomass."

"Are you sure?" Capn Jacq said. She didn't say, Not everyone is here.

"Yes. I'll take one more visual 360 then I think we'll have to declare it done."

Capn Jacq rubbed her face. She was a sailor from a long line of sailors. And life on the sea, the sea of space, was the only life she could tolerate. The sea ate sailors, it always had. No knowing how many had lost their lives at sea.

But not Phil. She couldn't accept that. Not Phil.

The deck doors closed out the fractals and the darkness of space.

Capn Jacq eased back in her command chair. She read the list of names again. Phil's identification hadn't come up. Sooner or later a Guard yacht would collect the floating bits of the *Beowulf*. Phil's DNA would be found in the debris. Until then the uncertainty would be hard to bear.

She closed her eyes.

When she opened her eyes again the lights were gone. The window displays were dark. The background whine of engines and motors had ceased. The rhythmic creak of an old spaceship reached overwhelming tones. The power was out.

She leaned against the desk. Emergency power would come up quickly. Blue light flicked on. The displays sprang back up. Navigator Rex flickered in his usual spot.

The hatch to the comm deck jerked open, crying a metallic protest. Marco used his legs to jam it all the way home.

"What's going on, Captain?" He stood uncomfortably in the hatch. "Why's the ship nonfunctional?"

Capn Jacq glared at Rex. "Yeah, Rex, why's *my* ship nonfunctional?"

"Best I can tell," Rex said, "fractals are lining the hull and might have broken out the antenna from its channel. Also, somehow, they shorted out the hull magnetosystem, which is why we're dark. But we're not nonfunctional.

"We're *not* nonfunctional," he repeated. "Some of the internal systems are fine: air, windows, even certain areas of propulsion. Not that I'd recommend going anywhere right now."

"All right," she said. "So we're in an overcrowded dark ship with nine extra crew. Send a couple of droids out to clear the hull. Marco knows how to fix the magnetosystem, right? He can fix the antenna, too. We have spares? Doesn't matter if we don't, has to be repaired.

"I don't suppose," she paused and then settled herself in her chair, "I don't suppose you got an SOS out? Anyone else know we're here?"

"Yes, I have a couple of fleet vessels coming and a Guard yacht says it's on the way. Might be a while. Captain Ada and Captain

Sven said they'd be here soonest. You have friends in the fleet. They'll help you with this. With Phil."

"Mind your own business!" she snarled. "What are you waiting for? Let's have some action!"

"Yes, ma'am," he said.

"I'll see to the survivors," she said. "Maybe they know...." She pursed her lips.

***

Capn Jacq stared out the true window at the wreck of the Beowulf. The ship appeared rearranged, not destroyed, missing a hunk of stern here and adding irregular portholes. Ice diamonds sparkled as they orbited the ship, particles of atmosphere vented and frozen.

"You can't go over there," Rex said.

"The survivors didn't see him abandon ship. He wasn't out there, we'd have found him. He has to be on the ship. I'm going."

"Think about your duties here," Rex said reasonably. "The fleet services will be here soon enough to help search for him but for right now you have to secure your own ship. We still haven't completed the repairs."

She laughed. "Get to it, then, and I'll get to finding Phil."

"You can't leave me in command. I'm a holo. It's illegal."

"Second officer is Marco. Can you handle taking orders from him?" Capn Jacq sat on the edge of her seat. She wanted to go. Now.

"Take him with you. Marco. I can work with the third mate. You have to buddy, you can't go over alone."

"No, not Marco, you need him for repairs. I'll take the green-horn. Mackenzie."

Rex rolled his eyes. "We don't have an umbilical set up. Hell, there's nothing secure to hook it to. You need someone with experience to go open space with you."

"You saw her this morning. She did fine." Capn Jacq stood up, flexed her shoulders. "Hail her for me."

Rex flicked the comm link. "Hey Mackenzie, ready for something new?"

***

"We'll be fine," Capn Jacq said.

Mackenzie's breathing rasped. Several hundred meters of open space separated the hatch deck of the *Northern Star* from the wreck of the *Beowulf*. The fractals had cleared, mostly, and the bits of asteroid debris had spun away. Somewhere out there were constellations, stars. Closer was the moon. The earth somewhere below. Mackenzie's head buzzed. Dizzy. She tried to find a point of focus.

"Keep your eyes on the structure, it's better that way," Capn Jacq said. "The sky will wait, but Phil is running out of time. We gotta get to the *Beowulf* now."

"Captain Phil?" Mackenzie said. "We're going for Phil?" She took a deep breath. "Where do we start?"

"Just dive," Capn Jacq said. She pointed inside the torn open hull of the ship. "Follow me," she said. "Aim for that breach."

Capn Jacq videoed the blasted structure as they approached. This section of the *Beowulf* was not airtight. An asteroid had only tapped the ship yet it tore apart like a glued-together model, with some parts shredding and some parts staying whole.

"I bet the below-decks are still air-tight," Capn Jacq said. "Down we go." She led her through the gangways, lifting her magnetic boots over the hatchways. Mackenzie followed her like a faithful dog, noting what was damaged and what was not, but mostly just making sure Capn Jacq was not alone.

The refrigerator, deep in the bowels of the ship, hummed.

"Still working," Mackenzie marvelled.

"Yeah, sturdiest machine in the ship. Keeps the fractals alive," Capn Jacq said. The mandelbrots moved around inside the fridge. "Needs more than loss of ship integrity to kill these damned things."

She slapped the ship's skin and punched a hole through the sheet aluminum. Shocked, she stared through the hull of the ship into open space. The ship was no longer reliable, no longer air-tight in repairable sections. The *Beowulf* was a derelict.

Fractals boiled in through the hole. In moments they filled the hold.

Mackenzie laughed. "Hey, they like me!" The fractals clung to her suit. She encouraged them to settle on her arms and torso.

"No!" Capn Jacq dove towards the greenhorn and tore the fractals from her suit. "If they lock edges they'll combine and compress. Squish you and eat you," she said. "Didn't they tell you about that?"

"No ma'am," Mackenzie said. She scrubbed a random fractal

away from her helmet. "I helped wipe down suits when crew came in from fishing but no one said. I didn't know."

Capn Jacq smacked her shoulder. "Don't get shook up. Learning is a good thing." She hailed the *Northern Star*.

"Cargo's still good," she said to Rex.

He asked when she wanted to transfer the refrigerated harvest.

"Send over a hose when you can spare crew," Capn Jacq said. "We'll need the haul to pay the bills." She thumbed off the comlink.

Mackenzie cleared her throat.

"What about a biomass scan?" she said. "That'd pinpoint his location for us."

Capn Jacq shrugged. "We tried that," she said. "No way to mask out the fractals. We'll have to do this visually, by the book. Most ships have a standard layout. *Beowulf's* no different. Just follow me."

Just outside the cargo hold, Capn Jacq stopped at an unlikely corner angle. "One of our favorite places." She pulled a bit at a top corner and the metal wall fell off into her hands. A closet space opened up in front of her. Empty.

"You really think Captain Phil might be here somewhere?"

"It's his ship. He wouldn't leave. Thing is, I'm the only one knows where all the secret places are," Capn Jacq said. "Me and Phil. I have to keep looking."

She popped open another bit of wall, this one a meter above deck level. Again, the space revealed was empty. "Two down, a hundred to go. You can go back, I'll stay."

"Not gonna leave you alone," Mackenzie mumbled.

"Good," she said. "I'd rather have someone along."

Mackenzie logged 500 feet of gangway and at least a dozen more hidey-holes.

"How can a ship have so many unlikely spaces?" she said. "Holes everywhere. It's bad design."

Capn Jacq coughed. "The *Northern Star* has a lot fewer spaces, it's a newer design. A lot less interesting."

Mackenzie sighed. "We're getting low on oxygen, Captain."

"What are you trying to say?" Capn Jacq stopped moving for the first time since they boarded the ship.

"We have to get back soon."

"If we're getting low, with our fresh oxygen tanks, then Phil is even closer to empty. I'm not leaving until I find him."

"Captain...."

"No!" Capn Jacq kicked at the gangway. "Not until I find him!"

She pulled up a bit of flooring parallel to the gangway. A pit was exposed, a coffin sized space between plastic girders. She swayed above the empty hole. She tumbled in.

"Capn? Is he there? Capn?" Mackenzie gazed into the hole. The captain didn't move. "Captain!"

She reached for the best grip she could get, a hand around the ankle, and yanked Capn Jacq out of the hole.

"Capn! Are you okay?"

The woman didn't respond. Mackenzie checked the facemask. Capn Jacq's eyes were closed. Her breathing fluttered.

"Aw god," Mackenzie said. She glanced at the o2 gauge. Not empty, but near enough. Capn Jacq had passed out.

She plugged her suit air into Capn Jacq's. Mackenzie's atmosphere drained as their suits equalized pressure. Not much oxygen was left on either of their gauges. Mackenzie swayed. Capn Jacq's voice restored her attention.

"Fridge," Capn Jacq said. "Airtight."

Mackenzie slipped her right arm around Capn Jacq. She dragged and shoved Capn Jacq down two levels to below decks and the refrigerator. The machine hummed.

She twisted the dogs on the hatch and pulled the portal open. Pressure blasted against her suit as atmosphere escaped. She shoved Capn Jacq through the hatch and followed, moving slow. She turned. A moment to seal the portal. The gauges showed pressure and chill. She thought slowly. The machine was still tight though a little short on pressure. Its engines churned as it worked to make up the difference. Fractals piled up in drifts around the hold. They didn't try to cover her like the ones in vacuum had. *Warmth*, she thought. *They're warm and docile.*

She pulled off her helmet and swallowed a lungful of air. Plenty of it. She coughed. Then she bent over Capn Jacq and struggled with her helmet's emergency release. After a moment the helmet came off.

Capn Jacq gasped for air, then sat up. Stared over her shoulder. Pushed her aside.

"Phil!"

She crawled to the wall. A white spacesuit gleamed through a pile of fractals. Capn Jacq dug into the pile and flung them away. She uncovered Phil in just moments.

"Phil!" She chafed his face.

Blood seeped through rips in his suit, frozen into rivulets of gore. A red emergency patch on his left leg sealed the suit at knee level. His leg was gone.

"Phil," she whispered. She cradled his head in her lap.

He opened his eyes. "I knew you'd come."

Mackenzie didn't want to see Capn Jacq cry. She turned her back on them and hailed Rex.

"You'll never guess who we found," she said. "And by the way, send someone to come get us, would ya?"

The Call of the Orbsong

A.M. Matte

Award-winning writer A.M. Matte
was first published at the age of 11,
and was a produced playwright by
the age of 12. Recent publications
include short stories in literary
magazines Virages and Ancrages
and collections Where Pigeons
Roost and other stories and Ce
que l'on divulgue. A.M. Matte is
currently working on a play, a novel
and a musical, with the support
of grants from the Ontario Arts
Council, the Toronto Arts Council
and the Canada Council for the
Arts. www.ammatte.ca

The orb in her mouth, Dafenid plunged, her long, lithe limbs pushing the water aside, enabling her to go deeper, deeper, where the Pavlina could not follow. Dafenid imagined her still on the shore, searching for her ball, mystified as to where it could have disappeared.

Dafenid knew this orb was special, the strongest evidence of which was that it was still warm and glowing gold despite being halfway in her throat. It was also obvious due to how enchanting it had sounded as the Pavlina played.

Dafenid veered west, away from the most populated areas of the pond and into a secluded marshland. The water was cloudy, with feathery hornwort plants obscuring the darkened spot that was her destination. It always gave Dafenid a thrill when she pushed aside the hornwort and sidled up to her cache. Though they no longer glowed, her mound of orbs was still beautiful.

She spat out her latest acquisition, placing the gold orb among the others, making it the fourteenth of her collection. She was pleased with herself and her accomplishment, until Luin swam up behind her.

"You have to stop this. The orbs mean a lot to her. She'll be upset when she can't find this one."

Luin's webbed fingers reached for the golden orb, plucking it from among its multi-coloured sisters. He turned it around, let it go, then caught it again, feeling its weight in his webbed palm despite the water's buoyant force.

"It's amazing what she can do with these." He glanced up at the mound of orbs behind Dafenid. "How can you bear to keep them here, silent?"

Dafenid snorted. Bubbles left her nostrils as she grabbed the orb from Luin and returned it to the top of the mound.

"She has so many," she said. "She won't miss this one just as she hasn't missed the others. You leave them be. They are mine, now."

Luin nodded, looking unsure, but Dafenid had made herself clear.

"She will get more. You will let me keep these orbs."

"You can't even play with them properly."

"One day, I'll learn."

Dafenid, whose Amphibian name was more difficult for Bipeds to pronounce (midway between Hroac and Rchbt), disapproved of her people's subordination to their dominant neighbours. Though it had long been granted independence, the Amphibian collective, known as the army, still behaved as if it owed its existence to the Bipeds, who only had the advantage of number, territory, and strength.

Dafenid remained a rarity as an Amphibian convinced of her species' superiority. Younger, she had envied the Bipeds' ability to grip with ease. Watching them play Orbit, the small vitreous orbs effortlessly landing and leaving their hands without so much as a slip, the Bipeds had seemed godlike to her. Later, when she came to appreciate her species' attributes—their easy, strong swimming and diving, their ability to breathe both on land and in the water, their ordered, peaceful coexistence—she knew the Bipeds were nothing special. The Pavlina was nothing special.

Dafenid took pride in the fact that Amphibian children did not need gimmicky toys to play. When they were little, Dafenid, Luin, their brothers and sisters played hide and seek in the reeds, played target practice by catching dragonflies with their tongues and then letting them go. Even as tadpoles, they raced, nipping at each other's tails in a rudimentary form of tag, and as froglets, played the obligatory leapfrog, allotting points to those who jumped highest and furthest.

Yet, somehow, the Pavlina playing Orbit trumped all of Dafenid and Luin's play and they spent more and more time watching the Biped master its species' latest trend.

The night Dafenid had stolen the golden orb, she and Luin had watched, mesmerized, as the Pavlina manipulated her orbs, fingers flickering through the air until the orbs' velocity and resonance lifted them out of her hands, which began to wave and weave amongst the polycarbonate spheres. As the Pavlina's concentration grew, the orbs picked up speed, dancing around her, with what was once a hum emanating from them growing into an eerie, intangible song. The gold orbsong was more beautiful than any they'd heard before.

Dafenid didn't know how long she and Luin watched and listened, the rapturous melody silencing even the birds, but it was past dusk when the Pavlina slowed her cadence, allowing the orbs to hover and glow about her head before she caught them in her hands again. Once the sun had set, the orbs' light shone brighter, compelling Dafenid to watch the Pavlina play her game as much as she observed Luin.

Where his gaze upon the young Biped had once been

amused—like hers—he now sat hypnotized as she displayed her skill at Orbit. Luin's large webbed fingers gripped the ground before him as his forelimbs supported most of his weight, edging unconsciously closer to the object of his affection.

Where Dafenid had merely felt a vague envy at the Pavlina's ability to manipulate the orbs—her own webbed limbs could not manage the intricate movements required to make the orbs dance and sing—Luin saw in the Pavlina much more than an expert gamer. Luin wasn't attracted to the Orbit gameplay; he was attracted to the player—an unthinkable taboo of which Dafenid made sure no one else was aware.

Dafenid cursed the enthralling orbs, with their glow and their song. She cursed the Pavlina's ability to play the game, the effortlessness with which she plied the orbs' course to her will. And, mostly, Dafenid cursed the evening she had first caught those aural tones on the wind.

They were young, then, she and Luin; even the Pavlina—who wouldn't master Orbit for years yet—was just a slip of a Biped. Nothing to suggest the alluring raven-haired and bronze-skinned exotic temptress she would become.

That night, the breeze had been warm and most of the army was content to laze on the pond banks and on the artificial waterlilies the Pavlina's family had provided when the pond had been designated protected territory.

It was barely noticeable at first. A wheezy, start-stop tune that was unlike any other sound or call they had heard around the pond before. Dafenid and Luin had agreed to investigate, intrigued by what was more than the wind whistling in the trees, but less than a linnet's cheerful song.

They left the pond and leapt toward the sound, stopping at the edge of the wood. Behind the willows' drooping branches, a young Biped was tossing coloured orbs in the air. As they fell, returning to her waiting hands, they made the sound Dafenid and Luin were listening for. After a few moments of observation, Luin declared he would go ask the Biped what she was doing, partly out of curiosity, partly to show off his self-taught ability to speak the Pavlina's language.

"Don't!" hissed Dafenid. "Let's just watch from here. We're far enough away that if she sees us, we can hop away."

But Luin was too captivated to heed her. He cautiously crept closer until he was but a few metres from the Pavlina.

"What is that?" Luin asked in broken Bipedian. (They claimed to have more than one language, but it was all the same gibberish to Dafenid.)

The Pavlina started.

"Who are you?"

He forgot himself and used his Amphibian name. The Pavlina's blank look reminded him of the Bipeds' need for alternate designations.

"I'm called Luin. You?"

"You may address me as Pavlina."

"Of course, Pavlina. I wouldn't presume—"

"Well, you did."

Dafenid bristled. She may not have understood most of the exchange, but she knew rudeness when she saw it. She called out to Luin, urging him to return to the pond. He ignored her croaks and inquired again, in his gravelly baritone, about the Pavlina's game.

Dafenid struggled to understand the Pavlina's speech, her voice like a bird's, tinkling in the air.

"Well, dolls are fine enough, if you like styling long bluegreen or fuchsia feathers, but Orbit is the thing to play now. New colours come out all the time, and the best players have a wider variety of orbs to play. I have the best collection of everyone I know."

She lifted her arms and began the dance again, the orbs slowly lifting away from her fingers into the air.

"The point of the game is to make the orbs float and sing as long as possible, as nicely as possible."

"Amazing," whispered Luin.

The Pavlina's pace faltered and the orbs dipped in the air. She tried to control the game and keep them hovering, but the four balls thudded to the ground, one by one.

"See what you made me do?" She sighed. "Make sure you don't bother me, next time."

Irritated by the Pavlina's dismissive tone toward her friend, Dafenid eyed a fallen ruby orb in the grass, and seized the opportunity. She flicked her sticky tongue out of her mouth and wrapped it around her glassy prey. Dafenid's tongue then snapped back, concealing the toy in her mouth.

Luin chattered all the way back to the pond, oblivious to Dafenid's inability to speak. It was several years and more than half a dozen stolen orbs before he discovered Dafenid's thievery. He didn't approve, but he didn't denounce her, either. He saw, from the way her lungs contracted, that she was both ashamed and proud of her stealthy exploits.

Dafenid had learned to control and to hide her emotions—as most of her family did. Both beauty and curse, inherited from her distant Lenidae ancestors, her translucent skin enabled any observer to literally see through her, her organs exposed. Now, unless she exerted a considerable amount of energy or was particularly frightened or shocked, her breathing and her heartbeat remained steady, as far as anyone could tell.

But Luin knew the subtle differences to watch for. He had noticed that Dafenid's skin turned a slight blue when she took the time to bask in midsummer sunshine. He knew the way her intestines tightened when she was displeased and, when this happened, he took care to distract her, to calm her down. He knew the difference between the speed of her heartbeat when she was surprised and when she was nervous—both of which were rare.

It was this attention to her every detail, this complete knowledge of her that had made Dafenid fall in love with Luin—an egotistical love that blossomed into a profound admiration and selfless love over the years.

Dafenid came to dream of a future with Luin. They had spoken of it once before, Luin wondering aloud if the army could be convinced that they were an ordained pair. Dafenid was thrilled at the thought, but in time, her feelings for Luin grew and what she hoped for was more than just an arranged pairing. To her, she and Luin were soulmates and their love would transcend their species' arranged mating tradition.

The tradition dated tens of suncycles back. It was important to the army that pairings be fruitful. As Amphibians evolved to be sentient and self-aware, and grew, in the short span of a few centuries, to over fifty times their original size, their ability to reproduce depleted. Genetics, therefore, dictated with whom one spent one's life, with the occasional exception allowed. Dafenid vowed to herself that she and Luin would be their generation's exception.

Dafenid believed that it was merely a matter of time before she and Luin were ordained. They already knew one another so well, already did everything together—it was no large leap to imagine the rest of their lives together. She could picture them finally voicing their devotion, swimming away to a corner of the pond to mate, hovering by their newly laid eggs, basking in the joy of creating a family. She felt that she would be an attentive mother, watching over their egg mass until their tadpoles hatched, tending the little ones as they turned into froglets, then into grown Amphibians. Luin would protect them and care for them, as a loving father would.

Dafenid didn't doubt her dream could come true. It was simply delayed while the Pavlina remained a distraction.

At first, Dafenid didn't mind Luin going off to play with the Biped. She understood the allure, the exoticism. She did mind that his focus remained on land when he came home.

"She showed me how I could move the orbs with sufficient velocity, with my tongue, to produce the beginning of a melody. She then played her orbs to match mine. Can you imagine?"

Luin's excitement was not contagious. Dafenid struggled to rein in her jealousy.

"She's just using you to make herself feel more skilled, more important," said Dafenid.

"We have to broaden our horizons, reach for better things, break down the barriers between our species," insisted Luin.

"It's a game!"

"It's a meeting of souls."

Dafenid swam away, confounded by Luin's irrational attachment to the Biped. She refused to speak to him for several days, hoping that he would come to miss her as he seemed to miss the Pavlina when she left their play for a few days.

Nearly a quarter mooncycle after the thievery, there was a commotion on the shore. Dafenid, swimming laps and snacking on diving beetles, saw her fourth sister talking animatedly with someone just behind the tall reeds. Her sister nodded, then plunged, only to emerge a few seconds later right next to her, her skin an excited tinge of yellow.

"Have you seen Luin? The Pavlovo is looking for him."

"The Pavlovo?"

Dafenid's skin rippled blue in shock. She calmed herself.

"The Pavlovo is here? Why would he want Luin?" She gasped. "This is the Pavlina's fault!"

Dafenid's sister nodded.

"She's definitely involved. She's here, too."

Again, Dafenid's skin rippled, this time less perceptibly.

"He's at the far marshland. I'll tell him."

Dafenid plunged, a swirl of thoughts in her mind as she pumped her legs in a rush to get to the other end of the pond. Did the

Pavlina finally deduce as to the whereabouts of her lost orbs, mistakenly believing Luin to have stolen them? Was the Pavlovo here to exact Bipedian justice in retaliation? Would he break the truce his family had upheld for generations? Over this?

Dafenid spotted Luin through the water, recognizing his speckled legs among those of his brothers' and friends'. She swam up to him and brushed against his arm. She knew that when he turned around, he would notice her heartbeat and immediately know that something was amiss.

"Hrchoacbt! What is it?"

He took her aside and put a forelimb around her. She basked in his affection for a brief moment before sharing the news.

"It's the Pavlovo. He's here, looking for you."

Luin was alarmed.

"The Pavlovo? Did something happen to the Pavlina?"

Dafenid shook his arm off her.

"Really? That's your concern? Our powerful neighbour, on whose goodwill we rely, comes with a retinue to ask for you, by name, and you're worried for her?"

She couldn't hide her disgust. He saw her intestines throb and changed tactics.

"Thank you for letting me know he's here. I'm sure it's nothing," he added, gently.

"Maybe you should hide..." she suggested.

"That won't do any good. Where else would I be but in our pond? Let's just go and find out what's going on."

Dafenid nodded and they swam back to the shore, Luin's brothers and friends, who had overheard, following closely behind. Dafenid was reassured by their presence. If Luin were threatened, surely the army would protect him.

They emerged together a few meters from the shore and Luin asked them to stay back as he made his way up to the Pavlovo, who was surrounded by his retinue of Bipeds. Luin was nervous, but attempted to hide it; he had spotted the Pavlina a few paces behind her father and he did not want to appear weak in her presence.

"And so, you are the one we call Luin."

The Pavlovo stated; he did not question. Luin nodded.

"I understand you have become friends, of sorts, with my daughter."

Luin nodded again. Dafenid was breathing heavily, but she tried to keep her anxiety from showing through. She was frightened for Luin. What would she do if the Pavlovo tried to harm him?

"I also understand that she has insulted you most egregiously, by refusing to keep a promise she made."

"Oh, Father," the Pavlina sighed irritably, her usual birdsong voice sounding more like summer crickets. "Must you cause me this humiliation?"

The Pavlovo turned to face her.

"Your family has not raised its daughter to bypass a promise and to disrespect its neighbours. Did young Luin here return an item dear to you?"

Dafenid's intestines seized in shock as she snapped her head to stare at Luin. I'm sorry! he mouthed at her. Dafenid realized that her beloved had ignored her wishes and brought the prized golden orb back to its owner.

"Yes, Father," the Pavlina grudgingly answered.

"And did you or did you not promise him a reward for the deed?"

"Yes, Father."

"Then I must insist that you uphold your end of the bargain. Please issue your invitation again, that Luin may accept it—if he so sees fit."

The Pavlina clenched her fists and marched regally up to Luin, who tried to puff his body out in order to look as tall and imposing as possible.

The Pavlina took a breath. She unclenched her fists and broke into a dazzling smile that changed her entire face. Luin gazed up at her, slack-jawed, while Dafenid seethed. What was the point of all those teeth the Pavlina had? Surely the Bipeds could do with just a few for sustenance?

"Luin," began the Pavlina, her tinkling voice higher than usual, yet perfectly audible despite the bristling reeds. No one else dared utter a sound.

"Luin, as previously agreed, please accept an invitation to my palace, where we will share our meals and my suite, to acknowledge the gallant act you performed when finding and returning my gold orb."

Luin's eyes blinked a few times before he was able to respond, the momentous occasion not lost on him.

"Thank you, Pavlina, I readily accept."

The army broke in crashing applause, their webbed fingers enthusiastically slapping the water in support.

"Furthermore," thundered the Pavlovo above the noise, "I extend the invitation to a full mooncycle, to make up for the promise that should not have been reneged."

"Father...!"

"Thank you, your Honour, I am most humbled," said Luin.

And Dafenid knew. Luin would leave the pond, leave the army, leave her—and she would never see him again. If anyone had been looking at her, they would have seen her heart break.

"Splendid!" cried the Pavlovo. "Let us depart."

Luin, as puffed up as he could be, hopped alongside the Pavlovo as he proceeded to his palace.

Turn around, just once! pleaded Dafenid to Luin's receding silhouette. She stared in the direction of the procession long after they had disappeared from sight.

"He'll be back soon," soothed her sister. "He'll have so many stories! Imagine: an Amphibian living at the palace!"

Dafenid nodded numbly, her skin feeling cold for the first time in her life. It was a disagreeable sensation that rivaled the disappointment and sadness she felt at being betrayed and bereft by the choices that Luin made.

She had but one ray of satisfaction left. At the bottom of the pond, thirteen orbs remained hers. The Pavlina may have her precious golden orb and the companionship of the sincerest Amphibian there was, but she was missing a sizeable amount of treasure.

Without a word to her sister, Dafenid plunged into the cool water. She pumped her powerful legs and reached the depths of her hiding place within seconds.

If Luin had returned to the pond, he would have found his first love behind the hornwort, atop a pile of extinguished orbs, which he could see both underneath and through her. Dafenid would bare her tongue and protect her mound, spreading her webbed limbs across it, as a mother guards her eggs.

"Orr-bit! Orr-bit!"

She would be incapable of saying anything else, and he would have to swim away, mystified at the power of the orbsong, which enthralled all who encountered it, even in the depths of silence.

Thank You

Many thanks to our patrons
and supporters, especially:

Cathrin Hagey

GriffinFire

Julia Patt

J'nae Spano

Knetti Eaton

Lian Fournier

Maria Haskins

Natalie Weizenbaum

Tory Hoke

zennjenn

Want to see your name here? Become a patron!
patreon.com/lunastation

About the Cover Artist

Kmye was born in April 1985 in France, and has been attracted to drawing, painting and all sorts of crafts since a very young age. She started displaying her artwork on the internet for fun in her late teens while pursuing her biology studies. These days she works as a scientist by day, but come night Dr Camille transforms into Ms Kmye in pursuit of mischief in general and art in particular. She has been working as an artist and freelance illustrator as time permits since 2008, and her work has been exhibited in group and solo shows across Europe and the US. She currently resides in Cambridge, UK.

Kmye is a proud member of the artist collective Copycat Violence.

You can find more of her work at:

kmye-chan.com